'How fortunate they [...] the betrothed couple. [...] strangers.'

The person she said [...] had come to stand beside her. She immediately felt the awkwardness of her words.

'You married a stranger very successfully,' he pointed out. 'I don't know what you have to complain of.'

They eyed each other with a latent hostility, and each felt the smart of an old grudge. He thought, *'She was a cunning little piece, even at fifteen. For how else did she contrive to put me off with a mask of dull indifference, while ensnaring the eligible Martin with soft glances from those remarkably beautiful eyes?'* She thought, *'How heartless he was, at a time when I needed kindness so badly.'* And each had a wicked desire to make the other fall a little in love.

If she could be taught to recognise what she had lost—if he could be made to admire what he had despised—how satisfying such a revenge would be . . .

Sheila Bishop was born in London and spent a wandering childhood while her father was in the regular army. She lived in South America for several years and had twice been through the Magellan Straits before she was nine. Later she returned to England, living first in the country and later in London and Essex. She worked as a short-hand typist with the Foreign Office and during the war did secretarial and welfare work with the British Red Cross Society, spending some time in North Africa and Italy—where she met her husband. They live in Bath, Somerset, and have one daughter. She likes to spend her free time visiting historical buildings where she sometimes acts as an official guide.

Sheila Bishop has written many Regency and Elizabethan romances. *True Lovers' Knot* is her first historical romance to be published in the Masquerade series.

# TRUE LOVERS' KNOT

## SHEILA BISHOP

**MILLS & BOON LIMITED**
15–16 BROOK'S MEWS
LONDON W1A 1DR

First published in Great Britain 1986
by Mills & Boon Limited

© Sheila Bishop 1986

Australian copyright 1986
Philippine copyright 1986
This edition 1986

ISBN 0 263 75367 0

Set in 10 on 11½ pt Linotron Times
04–0386–61,200

Photoset by Rowland Phototypesetting Limited
Bury St Edmunds, Suffolk
Made and printed in Great Britain by
Cox & Wyman Limited, Reading

# CONTENTS

# I

## *The Heiresses*

# CHAPTER ONE

'BUT WHO is Mrs Bridget Montresor?' asked Lucy Barnes timidly, gazing round the private upper room of the Salisbury inn, a replica of so many other inns where they had broken their journey to sleep or dine or rest the horses on the interminable ride west.

'She is the gentlewoman who is to escort you the rest of the way to Waldon Harbour,' Mr Phillips reminded her.

Although this did not exactly answer Lucy's question, she felt she might have known more about Mrs Montresor if she had paid proper attention, so she did not like to go on asking. For what difference could it make, after all? Nothing could render her life less wretched than it was already.

She was miserable and terrified. She had been in this state for several weeks and her bewilderment had one advantage; it had dulled the pain of a stronger grief for the death of her father.

She had loved him dearly. She was his only child, and after her mother's death they had meant everything to each other. Robert Barnes had been a lawyer, a clever boy who had gone to Cambridge as a poor scholar and made his way in the world. He had made money too, but hard work had been his chief passion and they had lived very quietly in his house near Blackfriars, seeing little company. Their closest friends had been a family called

Thompson who lived across the way. Mr Thompson was also a lawyer, harassed and less successful than Mr Barnes, with six children to provide for. It was the Thompsons who had taken Lucy in on the dreadful day of her father's seizure and she had accepted this refuge without question, too stunned to think about the future.

Then it turned out that her father had left more money than anyone expected, and had invoked the help of one of his powerful legal friends to protect her from the rapacity of those who might hope to get hold of her fortune. Could he really have meant the kind, unassuming Thompsons? At all events they had become proud and prickly, making no attempt to argue when Sir Rowland Hanson announced that he had arranged a marriage for her with a young gentleman called Giles Omberley and that she was to meet him at a great house in the country belonging to Sir William Rydal, who was Mr Omberley's godfather and had now been appointed her guardian.

It was the summer of 1592, and Lucy was not yet sixteen. While her father lived, she had looked on her marriage as an event in the future, comfortably far ahead in the future. To be handed over at once to a stranger chosen by strangers was such a daunting prospect that she could not even think sensibly about what was going on around her.

'So you are in your sullen fits again, my fine lady,' said the ugly, grating voice of Mrs Phillips almost in her ear. 'Not used to being kept waiting, I suppose.'

Mr and Mrs Phillips were travelling to the West Country on business of their own, and had promised to convey Lucy part of the way. Mr Phillips was a hanger-on of Sir Rowland Hanson, and they had no connection with Sir William Rydal or Mr Omberley. In spite of knowing this, Lucy could not help feeling that Mrs Phillips's continued hostility was a sample of the sort of treatment she must expect in her new life. She shrank away, too sunk in despair to guess that the woman envied her wealth and fine prospects. She did not see herself as an object of envy.

She was small and undeveloped, not yet grown to her full height, and her breasts were almost flat. She was dressed in mourning, which did not become her, for she had the delicate colouring that was swamped by black. Her eyes were almost hidden by their swollen lids, and her light brown hair was dull from lack of brushing. Her attempts to stifle her misery did indeed make her look sullen. She was not in the least like a bride.

She turned her back on the room and stared out of the window. There were people down there in the street: a fur-gowned merchant in his doorway, self-satisfied and sleek; a whistling schoolboy; a man with a tray on his head, crying hot pies. Lucy wished she could change places with any of them, because they all looked as though their lives were securely anchored in accustomed places among familiar faces.

A small string of horses trotted into the forecourt of the inn. There were three liveried servants, one of whom had a woman riding pillion behind him, while another was leading a packhorse, but the most important person in the party was undoubtedly the lady riding side-saddle with a scarlet doublet cut like a man's above the flowing skirt of her habit. There was a good deal of noise and bustle downstairs, and then the door of their private parlour was opened and the lady from the riding party walked in, peeling off her gloves.

'I am Mrs Bridget Montresor,' she announced. 'And I do not at all understand who it is I have come to meet. Sir Rowland Hanson's letter was too brief to make the matter clear. Is there a Mrs Barnes here?'

She was addressing Mr Phillips, who made her a deferential bow.

'Mrs Lucy Barnes, madam. She has come from London and is travelling to Waldon Harbour in order to be married.'

'Good God,' exclaimed Bridget Montresor. She looked across at Lucy who was still by the window. 'Is that why you are going there? To be married?'

'Well may you ask, madam,' said Mrs Phillips, placing herself between them before Lucy could answer. 'You'd hardly guess she was bound for her wedding, the ungrateful little hussy. Going to make a great match, far above her deserts, and all she can do is sulk and refuse her food and think herself above her company. I should be sorry to see any daughter of mine give herself such airs.'

Bridget was still staring at Lucy. She spared one disdainful glance for Mrs Phillips, and said in a clear, hard voice, 'I doubt whether any daughter of yours would have much to give herself airs about.'

Lucy expected an angry retort, but to her surprise Mrs Phillips was actually cowed and her husband even more so. They fidgeted, and said they must be on their way. No attempt was made to detain them, although Lucy had enough self-command to thank them insincerely for taking care of her.

A moment later she was alone with Bridget Montresor. They examined each other in silence. Bridget was tall and slender with fine, aquiline features. She would have made a handsome boy. Her face was too strong for beauty, but her complexion was clear and vivid and the thick russet-coloured hair that floated on her shoulders seemed alive with vitality. She had the most brilliant hazel eyes Lucy had ever seen.

Abruptly she asked, 'Are you legally contracted to Sir William Rydal's heir?'

'I don't know,' said Lucy uneasily. 'I have to marry a gentlemen called Mr Giles Omberley. I don't know if he is Sir William's heir.'

'He isn't. The heir is Martin Rydal, the old man's nephew. I thought it was too good to be true.'

'Why do you say that?'

'Because I have been chosen for the exalted prospect of marrying Martin. Yes, my dear; we are both sacrificial victims. Are you a great heiress?'

'I don't think so.'

'Well, I am! And it is a damned impediment, let me tell you.'

One of the liveried servants brought in a flagon of wine and some little cakes, and asked respectfully whether Lucy would mind riding pillion behind Mrs Bridget's groom, there being no second side-saddle available. Lucy was thankful to hear it. She had made the first part of the journey travelling pillion and had no idea of continuing in any other way. She had never been taught to manage a horse on her own.

For the rest of the day the small company moved through a fair country which seemed to become more isolated with every mile. Hills became higher, roads steeper, valleys deeper, and sheep more plentiful, though the houses were fewer and farther between. The rare villages they passed through seemed snug and prosperous; even the cottages were built of stone. Though it was June, the may was still in flower, so that the trees and bushes looked as though they had been caught in a miraculous snowstorm. The spicy scent hung in the air, larks sang overhead. Lucy felt a fraction less unhappy, bumping behind the saffron-coated groom.

Bridget often cantered on ahead, making the most of

her freedom. Sometimes she vanished altogether, and then they would come on her, sitting very still on her grey horse, listening to the quiet sounds of the countryside and gazing into the distance. Sometimes she rode close to Lucy, talking in a friendly way but not saying anything important. It was clear she did not intend to discuss their private affairs in front of the men in livery who were, Lucy discovered, the servants of her brother-in-law, Mr Henry Banstead. The other woman in the party was Bridget's maid Mercy.

That night they slept at a hostelry in yet another country town. The two girls shared a bed, so now it was possible to exchange more facts and compare notes. Lucy was quite ready to pour out her life-story, pleased to have someone she could confide in, and giving away more about herself than she knew.

'Poor little soul, she's like a lost dog,' thought Bridget indignantly. 'No one has thrown her so much as a bone of real consolation since her father died. I dare say those lawyer friends were kind enough until the will was read; then they thought Barnes had insulted them, and no wonder. Barnes had been suspicious, like many self-made men. It was plain that he had risen from nothing and nowhere, and that was probably why he had done so little to find suitable companions for his daughter: he had been afraid that she might be snubbed by those above her in birth and fortune, or exploited by those below. Now he had died, leaving the task undone—how like a man!—and the wretched girl was being sold off to some fellow who needed money so badly that he could not afford to be particular about breeding or connections.'

Bridget herself was a good deal more reserved in what she said to Lucy. Everything she told was the truth, though not the whole truth. She and her elder sister

Mary were the surviving children and co-heiresses of Sir John Montresor, who had left them large estates in the county of Northampton. Since their father's death, Bridget, then fourteen, had been living with her sister, who was already married. She was twenty and had recently fallen out with her relations because they wanted her to marry a man she did not like.

'Was he very disagreeable?' asked Lucy sympathetically.

'He was a fat little toad and the last of a long line of impossible suitors. I wasn't prepared to marry a man just because he was a hunting crony of Henry's or someone he wanted favours from. So I wrote to the Court of Wards and sued for my livery.'

'What does that mean?'

'I said I wanted to keep myself and handle my own money. Once a girl is passed sixteen, her guardians can be forced to hand over her fortune. I decided that I could manage very well without the Bansteads. I don't need a husband or a guardian to tell me what to do.'

'But surely an unmarried woman cannot conduct her own affairs?' asked Lucy, genuinely surprised.

'Why not? The Queen does.'

'That's different. And she is very old.'

'Treason, my dear.' Bridget laughed in the darkness. 'She was not so old when she came to the throne. She was twenty-five. Still, I did not expect the liberty of a queen. I knew I must live under the protection of a married lady of good repute, but I did think I should be allowed to choose a sponsor from among my own friends.' She paused, tasting again the bitterness of discovering that she was no match for those used to wielding authority: men, and old men at that. 'Lord Burleigh has consigned me into the hands of Sir William Rydal, whom I never met in my life and who simply wants a rich wife for his nephew. I should have done better to stay where I was.'

'Lord Burleigh,' repeated Lucy, awe-struck. 'The Queen's great Minister? What has it to do with him?'

'Among other things, he is the Master of the Court of Wards: the court that administers the estates of those who come into a great inheritance during their minority. I was made a ward of the Crown when my father died, though it was decided I should live with my sister.'

'But I am not a ward of the Crown,' said Lucy. 'I am sure the Queen and Lord Burleigh have never heard of me. I am of far too little consequence.'

Bridget was inclined to agree, though she thought it would be unkind to say so.

'I don't know who can have made the match between you and this Omberley,' she admitted. 'Or what Sir William Rydal can be about, sending for brides by the bushel! I find the matter almost too strange to credit.'

She would have been gratified to know that at this very moment, a day's journey further west at Waldon Harbour, Sir William Rydal himself was thinking very much the same. He felt like a man who had prayed for rain and been caught in a thunderstorm.

# CHAPTER
# TWO

SIR WILLIAM was the head of an ancient family who had lived on the same land since it was part of the Kingdom of Wessex. He was fifty-five, though he looked older, lame and stooping a little, his face worn with the lines of intermittent pain, for he had never entirely recovered from the wounds he had received twenty years earlier, fighting with the English contingent at the Battle of Lepanto.

Twice married and twice a widower, he had no sons or daughters of his own, but he had brought up two children whom he held in great affection. Martin Rydal was his nephew, his dead brother's son; Giles Omberley, his godson, had been left a penniless orphan and brought to Waldon Harbour at the age of nine. The two boys had always been good friends. Sir William had sent them up to Oxford together, and then to the Inns of Court, for the study of the law was part of a gentleman's education. Now they were both twenty-three and back at Waldon Harbour, Martin learning to manage the estate, Giles making himself useful as one of the upper servants of gentle birth who were employed in such houses. In a grander establishment he would have been called the Master of the Horse.

On several occasions Sir William might have arranged a marriage for his nephew, but he had not done so. Martin's position was ambiguous: heir presumptive rather than heir apparent. For Sir William had gone on hoping that he might still have sons of his own. There was nothing to prevent him taking a third wife. Only gradually had he brought himself to face the fact that God did not intend him to have children.

He had lived with his first wife in great affection for nine years, and she had never conceived, which seemed strange, for all her sisters were great breeders. She had died of smallpox, and when he married again he had taken great care to choose a widow who had already borne children to her first husband. Once again he had been unlucky. Then there had been Bess, his plump, good-natured mistress. She had given him no children either, which was all to the good: no man wanted a tribe of bastards about the place. He had been somewhat disconcerted, all the same, after he pensioned her off and found a husband for her to discover that Bess was far from barren. She had had four fine boys in a row: he was forever coming across them, tumbling about in the lane when he rode past the mill at Waterlip. He was glad to see Bess happy, but could not help feeling she had made him look a fool. So he had more or less decided to acknowledge Martin as his heir, when the matter took on a seeming urgency.

After an evening in the nearby market town of Chelford, which they had spent drinking in the Saracen's Head, Martin and Giles had been inspired by some imp of mischief to go round to the house of Thomas Trabb the clothier, the leading merchant in the place, and sing love-songs under the window of Trabb's daughter Agnes, a blameless maiden of sixteen who was considered a beauty because she had the longest and fairest hair of any girl in Chelford and a face as pink and innocent as a wild rose.

The next day, Thomas Trabb was over at Waldon

Harbour, complaining pompously about the slight to his family and the slur on his daughter's virtue.

Sir William had been furious. It was bad enough having to conciliate Trabb, a man he disliked, without the consciousness that his nephew had behaved like a mannerless lout and that everyone in Chelford knew it. He sent for the culprits and ordered them to make a most humble apology. When he had got rid of Trabb, he rated them soundly.

'I have never been so discomforted in my life,' he told them in a voice of freezing displeasure. 'I had not thought I should ever hear such an account of your pleasures: swilling sack and talking bawdy with half the wildheads in Chelford and then going after Trabb's girl like a pair of tomcats. A worthy occupation for two gentlemen of birth and breeding! There is only one thing worse, let me tell you, than habitually drinking in taverns with men in a lower state of life than your own, and that is indulging in amorous antics with young women of a like condition.'

He had temporarily forgotten that of course Martin and Giles knew all about Bess Franklin; and neither of them dared to remind him. Suitably chastened, they had assured him they had no evil intentions towards Mrs Agnes Trabb, it had all been a piece of thoughtless folly.

He believed them. This sort of escapade would have struck him as fairly harmless when they were in London, eating their dinners at the Middle Temple, but Martin at twenty-three should have known better than to behave so stupidly on his own doorstep. That was when Sir William had finally decided to choose a wife for him.

He began to sift through in his mind all the great families in the county, trying to remember the ages and dispositions of the various daughters. The Gretton ladies at Idenbrook, for instance, or the Bolderston girls and others further afield. He soon realised that most of these were married or betrothed already. He was puzzled at first, and then chagrined as he grasped the reason. He had left it too late. The kind of girl he would consider as a suitable mistress for Waldon Harbour, a girl with money and connections, would have been spoken for in her early teens. So he had decided to apply for the guardianship of one of the wards of the Crown, this being a recognised way in which a man of wealth and position could arrange a good match for his heir.

'I think my petition will be granted,' he had confided to his steward, John Redfern, who was also an old and trusted friend. 'I've raised levies, sat in Parliament, and never asked much for myself in the past. And I am well acquainted with Sir Rowland Hanson, who is one of the Commissioners of the Court of Wards. He'll send me a likely heiress if he can. I only hope he'll have such an article at his disposal. I ought to have got the boy betrothed and wed long before this.'

John Redfern was attached to his master and anxious to reassure him. 'It would be a good thing for Mr Martin to be married. Though if you will forgive my saying so, I don't think he is in any danger of drifting into bad company or bad habits. I expect it was young Giles who was responsible for last night's imbroglio. He has a singular talent for playing the lord of misrule in or out of season. And Mr Martin goes along with him.'

'Martin has the stronger character,' said Sir William rather sharply. 'However, I take your meaning. Giles is inclined to be restless; Martin is good-natured, and they have always been inseparable.'

He wondered fleetingly how well Martin would settle down with a bride he hardly knew, if his lively friend was always about the place, tempting him back to the care-free amusements of his bachelor days. Yet it would be monstrous to send Giles away simply because he might prove a disturbing influence. He had no fortune of his own and no other patron he could turn to.

'It's a pity I can't apply to the Court of Wards for two heiresses,' he went on. 'Unluckily, Giles has no claim to put forward. Yet he needs a rich wife more than Martin does.'

John Redfern looked thoughtful. 'To be sure, Giles is not entitled to ask for one of the Crown wards, but it strikes me that Sir Rowland, placed as he is, might often hear of less exalted young women in need of husbands. There must be plenty of men of the middle sort who have made enough money to marry their daughters into the gentry and don't know how to set about it. I dare say he is sometimes asked to advise such people. Giles's birth is impeccable, and if you were to recommend him, sir, he might well be put in the way of making a prosperous marriage.'

'That's a very good notion of yours, John,' said Sir William approvingly. 'I'll write to Hanson after dinner.'

Now, six weeks later, he was a good deal disconcerted by the result.

'I never thought he'd send me two heiresses at once, let alone arrange for them to travel down together. I cannot help wishing . . . However, I must not be ungrateful.'

Once again Sir William was confiding in Redfern as they sat companionably in his oak-lined study behind the great hall at Waldon Harbour, each taking a pipe of tobacco and enfolded in his separate cloud of smoke.

'The awkwardness will soon be got over,' said the steward.

'Well, I hope so. My sister says we shall be the talk of the countryside.'

Sir William's widowed sister Lady Porter had lived with him since the death of his second wife. Redfern knew that his master paid scant attention to her opinions. That he was now repeating her words showed he had misgivings of his own. He also knew that these apprehensions were for his ears alone, and that in public Sir William would preserve an air of calm determination, certain that his wishes would be respected and that all his subordinates would do what they were told.


'I don't want to be married!' insisted Giles Omberley.

'Try not to tell my uncle so,' begged his friend, 'just for the present. You know what a bad effect it has on his temper to be thwarted.'

Giles eyed him with a challenging mockery. 'Afraid for your skin?'

'I'm afraid for those young women arriving here as strangers. The ordeal must be worse for them than it is for us. We don't want them meeting my uncle in one of his chilling humours.'

It was like Martin to consider the feelings of the unknown girls who were due to arrive next day. Giles had not given a thought to their predicament, being too intent on his own . . .

The two young men were very different, in looks and in character. Martin was tall and slim, with thick brown hair worn rather long and curling at the ends. His eyes were a luminous grey, and his regular features had a coin-like perfection. Giles was several inches shorter, dark and sturdily built. His face, alight with animation, was almost ugly. They were as close as brothers in spite of the contrast in their circumstances. There had never been the slightest hint of arrogance on one side or envy on the other, probably because Sir William had treated them exactly alike when they were children.

While their benefactor was seeking solace in tobacco, his two protégés had come out into the moonlit evening to stroll along the bank of the clear rushing stream which ran through Waldoncombe to become one of the tributaries of the river Chel just above Chelford. The bottom of the combe was wide and green. Some way over to their left, parallel to the stream, was the riding track which served as the only road to Waldon Harbour, with the parish church and a few houses strung along on the far side. The outer walls of the combe were shadowed with trees.

Giles stopped and threw a stone into the water.

'I can see why he wishes you to marry. But why should he concern himself with me? I don't need a wife.'

'He thinks you do—to save you from the lures of Venus! It's your own fault. I grant you we were both as pickled as herrings, but it was you who would go off at midnight to salute the fair Agnes with six verses of "Greensleeves"!'

Martin laughed suddenly.

'What do you find so diverting?' asked Giles with dignity.

'Your face, when the window opened, and instead of Agnes smiling down on us it was old Trabb with his piss-pot ready to empty on our heads. You'd have been drowned if I hadn't dragged you to safety just in time.'

Giles laughed too. 'Wasn't he angry? "Be off, you scoundrels or I'll set the dogs on you, and the constable!" Though I still can't make out how he knew it was us.'

'Half the town knew,' said Martin. 'I suppose that's what my uncle minded most.'

They had walked along the bank of the stream nearly

as far as the sawmill. They turned back and saw the heart of the combe, and rising out of the smooth turf, against an amphitheatre of hanging woods, the beauty of Waldon Harbour. Honey-gold by day and ash-pale in the moonlight, it had the effect of a perfectly set jewel. The present house, built by Sir William's father in the reign of Henry VIII, had never been fortified, though it retained the suggestion of a defensive ground-plan. There was much decorated stonework at the front, whereas the main part of the house was inward-looking, a hollow square shaped round a paved court which had to be approached through a formidable gatehouse.

As they walked back across the grass, Martin remarked, 'By this time tomorrow we shall know our fates.'

'Don't you dislike the prospect of having to marry a stranger?'

'I've grown accustomed to the idea. I've always expected I must look for this kind of marriage if my uncle made me his heir. She's a Montresor, and very accomplished, so we are told. Provided she has a good disposition!'

'What if she's a shrew? Twenty years old is rather late for a great heiress still to be seeking a husband.'

'Yes, I've thought of that: she may have been betrothed once already and her affianced husband died before they could be married.'

It was a consoling explanation and not unlikely. Giles decided not to tease him with any more gloomy prophecies. For himself, he was by no means resigned to the match Sir William had so kindly arranged for him, but would keep quiet at present and hope to see a way out of the snare.

The porter let them through the gatehouse, then they crossed the paved court and entered the building by the main door. The lights in the great hall had already been quenched. They moved quietly through the screen passage and up the stairs. They needed no candle, for they could find their way round Waldon Harbour in the dark. It was their home.

# CHAPTER
# THREE

ON THE following day Sir William posted a groom on the hillside above the combe to watch for the arrival of his two new wards. Half-way through the afternoon the man came galloping in to say that he had sighted a small riding party on the Chelford road.

'We'll meet them outside the gatehouse,' Sir William decided. 'They cannot be left to cross the quadrangle unattended. We must show them every courtesy. Come, Martin—Giles.'

'I hope you do not expect me to stand out there in the sun, William,' said his sister in a martyred accent.

'Certainly not, my dear. I will bring the young gentlewomen indoors to meet you.'

Lady Porter was large and sedate. Placid as a rule, she was annoyed with her brother for making these matrimonial plans without consulting her, and kept pointing out that the presence in the house of two unknown brides must strike their neighbours as quite outlandish. Everyone would think that Waldon Harbour was a nest of Turks! Sir William did not think that her reluctant presence would add much to the comfort of Mrs Montresor and Mrs Barnes when they first set eyes on their new home.

The three men waited on the turf in front of the gatehouse, bare-headed in the afternoon light. The riding party soon became audible and visible on the valley road. The leader was a grey ridden by a lady in a scarlet habit. Behind her they could pick out three liveried servants, one leading a packhorse.

'There's only one heiress!' exclaimed Giles hopefully.

He could see by now that two of the men had dumpy figures sitting up behind them, but took it for granted that these anonymous females were merely maid-servants.

Neither Martin nor Sir William answered. They were both keenly scrutinising the fine young woman on the grey, who must be Bridget Montresor. The presence of the liveried servants made that plain. Giles felt an immense relief. He was glad he had kept his feelings more or less to himself; he would not willingly hurt or offend his kind-hearted patron.

The small group had reached the gatehouse. Bridget Montresor reined in her horse and looked down from her superior height at the three men who gazed up at her, all with some degree of admiration.

Martin stepped forward to help her dismount. She slid gracefully through his arms. For a moment they were so close that they might have been embracing. Then she freed herself and turned to curtsy to Sir William, not an easy feat for someone who had just set foot on the ground after several hours in the saddle, but she acquitted herself perfectly. He was delighted with her and made his speech of welcome with real enthusiasm.

'It gives me great pleasure to see you at Waldon Harbour, my dear madam. I wish you may long remain here and find every cause for happiness. This young man is my nephew Martin, with whom I hope you will soon be much better acquainted. And now I must take you to meet my sister. You must be weary after your long journey.'

'You are very kind, sir, but I think it is Mrs Barnes who requires your solicitude more than I do. She is not so used to travelling.'

They all became aware that one of the grooms had helped his pillion passenger to dismount, and that she was not a serving-maid after all. Her clothes, though sombre and ugly, were too rich. Under the brim of her heavy hat they saw a pale, sullen face which showed no animation as she stumbled forward, reluctant and awkward.

'So this is the beauty I'm supposed to pair off with,' thought Giles, his hopes of escape suddenly dashed. He was furious.

If Sir William was astonished by the sight of his second ward, he hid the fact, spoke kindly to the girl and presented his nephew to her.

'And this,' he added with emphasis, 'is Mr Giles Omberley.'

Giles had enough courtesy to make her an adequate bow and murmur a civil greeting. This was no consolation to Lucy, who had seen his look of consternation when he first set eyes on her. She became quite speechless and did not open her mouth during all the ceremony of being brought into the house, taken upstairs and presented to Lady Porter.

When at last she was alone with Bridget, she said, 'It is worse than I thought.'

'Take heart, there is nothing to be afraid of.'

Which in the circumstances was foolish—there was everything to be afraid of, but the poor child must be given some kind of reassurance.

They were in the bedchamber allotted to Lucy, the last and smallest of a series of adjoining rooms overlooking the inner court. Bridget's maid Mercy was unpacking her cloakbag in the larger room next door, while Bridget was unpacking for Lucy, who sat on the bed, trying to stop the trembling of her hands.

'It is such a very great house,' she said, overawed.

'Well enough in a provincial style forty years out of date.' Bridget was deliberately disparaging, though she had been secretly impressed by the Arcadian setting, the splendour of the rooms she had seen so far, and the rich furnishings. 'I suppose we must now deck ourselves out in fine raiment. It is a pity you are obliged to wear mourning. I wonder whether you would care to borrow one of my embroidered stomachers, and a necklace, perhaps? It would not be disrespectful to your father's memory.'

She was anxious to make the girl show to better advantage, for poor little friendless Lucy really did need a husband to take care of her, so she might as well try to please the bridegroom she was offered.

'And after all,' she reminded herself, 'there is no reason why Lucy should not be happy. She isn't doomed as I am to misery and secrecy.' For an unguarded moment she looked back with horror and anguish and then resolutely slammed the door of her mind, as she always did on that particular memory. She offered to brush Lucy's hair, knowing that if Mercy was asked to do so she would be grudging and cross, for she despised the lawyer's daughter as someone beneath her notice.

Lucy was intensely grateful. Bridget had done so much to banish her sense of inferiority, and there had been a moment today as they rode through the valley when her fears had been almost submerged by the beauty of their surroundings, the golden house set against the green of the woods. She had seen the three waiting figures. The old gentleman was easily recognised, but there had been nothing to tell her which of the younger men was which. The tall one was very handsome with a bright, open expression; he looked both gentle and strong. She had felt an unexpected leap of hope, only to find that this was Sir William's nephew, the husband destined for Bridget. And so he should be, of course: they would make a peerless couple, worthy of the great house and the great family. Only the short, thick-set man, Giles Omberley, looked so angry and scornful—he had taken against her at the first glance. Even so, the ordeal of the next few hours had to be got through somehow.

A feast to celebrate their arrival had been set out in the great chamber, a magnificent room on the first floor. All the Rydal plate was on display: cups and mazers and other vessels of gilt and silver-gilt, and a salt in the shape of a casket supported by two dolphins. The dishes included a roast swan and a glazed salmon with a salad of lettuce and marigolds. The company sat with their backs to the wall and were served from the front by the gentleman-usher. Sir William sat in the centre, with his sister on his right and on his left Martin and then Giles. Bridget was on Lady Porter's right and, beyond her, Lucy. This formally correct arrangement had an advantage from Lucy's point of view: she was not required to talk to anybody. She was able to sit quietly and concentrate on her table manners, neatly manipulating a knife and a manchet of bread. In between mouthfuls she admired the vividly coloured tapestry, which told the story of Theseus and Ariadne, the high chimneybreast of alabaster, the ceiling encrusted with plasterwork as fine as Venetian lace.

Most of the conversation was carried on by Lady Porter, who was closely questioning Bridget about her family connections and other august persons. Bridget answered easily. She seemed to know everyone Lady Porter knew, and not to stand in awe of any of them.

When the main part of the meal was over, they all rose
and went through the long gallery into a small banqueting-room at the far corner. The array of small dishes laid
out for them there consisted of almond tarts and other
spiced delicacies, which were handed round while the
servants cleared and removed the table from the great
chamber. Lucy accepted a sugar-plum and moved to
look out of the window, as she had done at the Salisbury
inn, to avoid talking to the people in the room. What she
saw immediately below surprised and charmed her. It
was an enclosed garden, perfectly square and surrounded by a moat. Inside the moat was a pleached alley
composed of carefully trained shrubs and trees which
clambered all over an arcade of trellis-work so that it
looked from above like an immensely thick hedge.
Within the double barrier of water and branches was
another square, the garden itself, quartered and sub-
divided round a central fountain. Some of the tiny plots
had flowers in them, some had herbs, and many were
planted with little box hedges wound round to themselves in intricate designs.

'How pretty it is!' Lucy exclaimed, pleasure over-
coming her shyness. 'I never saw anything like it before.'

'You have not lived in the country until now?' asked
Giles, addressing her for the first time.

'No, never.'

He was no longer frowning, and though she still
thought him rather ugly, with those thick black eyebrows, she realised that he was younger than she had
imagined. She decided to risk a question which had been
puzzling her ever since her arrival.

'How far off is the sea? I thought we should be on the
coast.'

'On the coast? Good God, no! We're forty miles
inland,' he replied scornfully, as one who would say, are

you really such a fool that you have travelled right across England without knowing where you were going?

Lucy flushed painfully. Martin, on her other side, said, 'I expect you were misled by the name of the house. It is an easy mistake. We believe it comes from the Latin word *arbor*, which means . . .'

' "Waldon in the trees!" That is just what it ought to be called. How stupid of me, I might have guessed.'

Martin smiled. He was surprised to find that she knew some Latin. But Giles had turned away and did not hear.

The shearing season was just over, and on the following day Sir William announced that they would all attend the sheep-shearing feast which was held every June for the shepherds and their families and all the other people on the estate.

Lady Porter thought this a false move. 'That young madam will take us for a sad pack of rustics.'

Sir William did not agree. He did not think Bridget Montresor was either haughty or affected, and in any case he wanted to make it plain that the future mistress of Waldon Harbour, however great her wealth and consequence, had a primary duty to concern herself with her husband's home and his dependants.

The feast took place every year in a flattish meadow on the far side of the stream.

'How many sheep have you, sir?' asked Bridget as they made their way across the bridge. She was walking between Sir William and Martin, addressing the knight and ignoring his nephew.

'Around seven thousand, so far as we can count.'

The greater part of his income lay in wool, surpassing what he received in rents.

A large party of country people had assembled in their

best clothes, and there were tables laid under the trees, loaded with hams and cheeses and custards, jugs of ale and bowls of cream. The older men and women moved towards the benches, ready to sit down in happy expectation, but two men with ribbons in their hats began to play a dance-measure on the pipe and tabor, and the younger shepherds, ploughboys and milkmaids decided to start dancing straight away. As they formed into circles, Martin saw Bridget watching them, her foot tapping to the rhythm of the jig.

On a sudden impulse he said, 'Would you like to join them?'

She looked at him thoughtfully and then laid her hand on his arm. Town-bred Lucy was rather surprised to see them walk off into the throng of villagers. Were she and Bridget supposed to join in these country revels? And, if so, would Giles Omberley claim her as a partner? She hoped not, for she was sure she would disgrace herself in some way, and he would despise her. Giles, however, was talking to some of the men, and never looked in her direction. She sat on a bench beside Lady Porter's waiting-gentlewoman, and no one else came near her.

Sir William did not notice her. His eyes were on Martin and Bridget as they swung through the set, perfectly at ease because they had each been brought up in a great country house and knew how to conduct themselves.

'That girl knows how to make herself popular among the tenantry,' he thought, 'without sacrificing an inch of her dignity or their respect.' He was very pleased with her. If he had been twenty years younger, he would have married her himself.

When the dance was over, the young people drifted towards the tables. They would dance again later, but now they were hungry and thirsty. Martin and Bridget had already dined at the great house. Finding themselves some way along the meadow beyond the feasting place, they moved into the shade. It was pleasant to be in the shadow of the wooded hillside.

'You have a good deal of timber here,' she said, studying the trees. 'Coppice oaks, I see. Have you a tannery?'

'Downstream towards Chelford. We don't get wind of it here.'

He was impressed by her knowing what the small oaks were there for: the bark was essential for tanning hides.

She stepped into the wood and stood looking about her. There was a patch of white windflowers near her feet, and a few wild hyacinths still remained, ghostly blue in their transparency. And she fitted the scene very well in her embroidered linen kirtle, her hair a bright cloud over her shoulders. Perhaps this was the moment to begin his courtship.

'I believe you are as much interested in country pursuits as I am,' he said. 'It is a good omen, do you not think?'

'An omen of what, Mr Rydal?'

'Why, of our—our future dealings together.'

He was surprised that she did not respond to his opening gambit. He hoped she was not going to be coy—that did not seem at all in her character. And she had not sounded coy, merely indifferent and a little impatient. Was she annoyed because he had not begun with a string of compliments, or tried to kiss her? An ugly woman might have been hurt by his prosaic approach, but surely this handsome girl did not need to be told how desirable she was, or how ready he would be to play the lover as soon as she allowed him close enough? In fact it was the sense of something cool and withdrawn about her that was holding him off. She still made no attempt to help him out, and there was an awkward pause.

So he tried again, this time without finesse. 'Since we are to be married . . .'

'You are jumping to conclusions, sir. I have not said I will marry you, and I may as well tell you that I don't mean to.'

He stared at her. 'How can you say so? We are as good as betrothed. If you did not wish to marry me, why did you come here?'

'Because Lord Burleigh placed me in your uncle's charge, and I had no choice.'

She looked perfectly composed as she said this, standing a few feet away from him, her face pale, her voice resolute. He wondered whether she was telling the truth. There were stories of unwilling daughters being forced into marriages by ambitious parents, but it was hard to see who could have tyrannised over Bridget in such a way. Old Lord Burleigh was a pattern of morality, and no official at the Court of Wards stood to gain anything by arranging this match. A new idea struck him.

'Are you already . . . Have you given your promise to some other man?'

She laughed, a little sharp laugh like broken glass. 'That is the only impediment a rejected suitor can ever recognise. We are all supposed to be in thrall to one of your sex. I am sorry to disoblige you, Mr Rydal, but I am not contracted to anyone else, nor likely to be.'

She walked out of the wood, and he followed, some way behind her and not attempting to catch up. He hoped no one had noticed them going off together, or the distant and unfriendly manner of their return. Luckily the ale had been circulating, and the revellers were intent on enjoying themselves.

Bridget went over to join Lucy, who was looking very forlorn. Martin remained on the outskirts of the festivities. Someone handed him a pot of ale and he drank it morosely.

His encounter with Bridget had left him feeling stunned. In all his life no one had ever dealt him such a blow. Whatever she might say, he was convinced that she had come down here intending to marry him, and for some reason had taken such a dislike to him that she had changed her mind. He did not think he was vain—though in fact he would have had to be almost inhuman not to be aware of his own good looks, talents and privileged position. He certainly did not give himself airs or exaggerate his own consequence. He had not expected her to fall in love with him at first sight. He was not in love with her, for that matter. He did not really admire tall women. But nature had done well enough for each of them to please the other; and that, combined with so many practical advantages, ought to be a firm enough foundation for the trust and affection which would grow with time. Yet she had turned him down flat, not through virginal diffidence— he could have understood that. She had seemed to take pleasure in refusing him, and that was truly humiliating. What was there about him which she found so repugnant?

He continued to brood for the rest of the day, in such a state of wounded pride that when Giles asked him what progress he was making with Mrs Montresor, he could not bring himself to tell the truth at first, even to his closest friend.

Instead, he turned the tables by saying, 'I don't see you paying much attention to your girl. You might show her a little kindness.'

'She is not my girl. I am not bound to her in any way,

which is a very good reason why I should keep my distance. No point in raising false hopes.'

'But what's to become of the poor child?'

'Ask your uncle. He brought her here, not I.'

After a moment's thought, Giles added, 'I dare say your wife will take her as a waiting-woman and give her a little polish. She has a comfortable dowry; she'll not die an old maid.'

'You are very ready to make plans for others. There is one obstacle, however.' Martin nerved himself to admit the painful truth. 'I shall not be getting married. Bridget Montresor has made it plain that she won't have me.'

Giles gazed at him in disbelief. 'She must be mad!'

'I thank you, my dear fellow.' Martin managed a faint smile. 'You have restored me in my own conceit.'

The two ill-assorted couples remained in limbo for another day. Martin had a respite from dancing attendance on his unbiddable heiress. News had reached the great house of a fire at one of the manors, and Sir William sent Martin to talk to the tenant and inspect the damage.

When he returned to Waldon Harbour in the middle of a hot afternoon, the place had seemed as deserted as an enchanted castle in a fairytale. The servants told him that Sir William had taken Mrs Montresor to see the newly enclosed fields at Higher Waldon. 'She is taking an uncommon interest in the estate,' thought Martin sourly, 'for someone who is determined not to marry the heir!'

He went out and stood absently gazing into the moat which ran round the enclosed garden. It was fed by the stream, so it was lively and clear, well stocked with carp. They always had fresh fish to eat. There was a boat tied up near the little bridge: he got into it and picked up the oars. A couple of strokes took him across to the other side, where he could drift lazily in the shade made by the dense pleached alley. It was cool, calm and peaceful, balm to his lacerated spirit, and he was lying back, trailing his hand in the water, his mind almost vacant, when he was assailed by a sound inside the garden: the sound of someone crying, in a monotony of wordless, hopeless despair.

Martin sat up and listened. He knew where the sound was coming from. There was a small bower at each corner of the garden, and in the most remote of them someone had gone to weep undisturbed. It was not difficult to guess who this might be. Ought he to respect her desire for privacy? He thought not. He slid the boat silently to a place where there was a ring to which he could make fast. Then he stepped ashore, found one of the half-concealed openings in the pleached alley, and entered the garden. He walked along under the tunnel of branches until he came to the corner. Even before he reached the bower, he saw between the fresh green interlacing of the leaves the expected smudge of black.

Beyond, in the small enclosure, was Lucy Barnes in her deep mourning, sitting on the ground with her head and shoulders propped against the stone seat, crying like a child.

He stood looking down at her. She did not seem to have heard his footsteps on the flagged path.

At last he said, 'I am afraid you must be very unhappy. Can I help you?'

Lucy jerked round with a gulp of fright and tried to scramble to her feet. 'I—I am sorry,' she stammered. 'There is nothing—I did not mean—I am sorry.'

She looked terrified, as though he might be angry with her for daring to be unhappy, when she had come to his uncle's fine mansion to marry his friend and ought to be in raptures.

'I expect you are homesick,' he said. 'Come, let us sit down and you can tell me. Is that what is wrong?'

Docile, she sat beside him on the bench. The tears had stopped, her voice was low and husky. 'I have no home. There is no one, no one at all, since my father died.'

Her recent bereavement made the flood of tears seem more natural and removed some of the awkwardness. He asked about her father, and she began to talk about him with complete simplicity, and about the small house in London where she had lived all her life, safe and content. Martin encouraged her, being careful not to look at her directly, for he thought she would not like to be stared at after crying so much. Instead, he kept his eyes on her hands as they lay in her lap. Beautiful hands they were, white and narrow, with long fingers and nails shaped like almonds. Her voice was pretty, too, in spite of all the tears. The home she described, though very unlike his own, had certain similarities. There had been order and affection and a high value set on learning and accomplishment. Mr Barnes had seen to it that his daughter was well educated: he had employed good masters to teach her and given her the run of his library. He had also left her all the money he had earned in his hard-working life and never had time to spend. Martin came to the conclusion that he had equipped her to marry a gentleman and move in wider circles than their own, but had never shown her the world outside that one small house. No wonder she felt bewildered.

'You are bound to feel your father's death more than most daughters, having no other kith or kin,' he said. 'So it is a good thing you have come here to make new ties.'

'What sorts of ties? They told me I should be married,

but it is not so. Mr Omberley does not want to marry me.'

'You are mistaken,' said Martin, and was ashamed of his insincerity, for he knew she was right.

Apart from not wanting to marry anyone, Giles had not been attracted by this timid and very young girl, and had made his feelings so plain that she had recognised them, ignorant as she was. No wonder she felt desolate. Angry with his lifelong friend, Martin tried to explain away his churlish behaviour.

'It is not easy for a man to meet his future wife for the first time. Giles has not appeared at his best. He is a splendid fellow, and you will soon learn to like him as you get to know him better.'

'But I don't think he will learn to like me,' said Lucy, seizing on the real flaw in this argument. 'I am not beautiful or well born or versed in witty conversation, and I am sure he is too impatient to put up with a dull wife.'

Martin thought this showed remarkable perception from someone who had spent the last few days with her eyes on the ground, apparently blind and deaf to everything that was going on around her. For she had certainly summed Giles up. If they did marry, he was so quick and thoughtless that he would probably be unkind to her without even meaning to be. He would certainly be unfaithful. It was a wretched business.

'I hope Sir William will not be very much displeased at my not being the sort of wife he wanted for his godson,' continued Lucy. 'Though it is your marriage that is bound to be his chief concern after all, and one can tell how delighted he is with Bridget, Mrs Montresor.'

Martin had almost forgotten his own predicament. When it came back into his mind, he had a sudden and surprising impulse to let Lucy know how things stood. 'I am afraid my uncle is going to be disappointed. You and I are companions in adversity. You have convinced yourself that Giles doesn't want to marry you, and I have it direct from Mrs Montresor that she doesn't want to marry me.'

'Has she told you so?' exclaimed Lucy. 'I did hope she might have changed her mind.'

She raised her drooping head and looked straight at him, so that for the first time he had the chance of noticing her eyes, which in spite of their swollen lids were very large and a most entrancing colour: a deep violet blue. He was so fascinated by this revelation that it took him a moment to decipher what she had just said.

Then he asked, 'Was she set against this marriage from the start? Did she tell you so before we met?'

'Not in so many words. I think she was angry that anyone could compel her to accept a husband she had not chosen. She said that women should be allowed to remain single. But after we came here, I thought she must soon be reconciled to the idea of becoming your wife.'

'I fear she still remains adamant.' Martin spoke quite cheerfully, for he now realised that Bridget had not been put off by any particular defect of his.

'I cannot understand her,' said Lucy. 'How can she throw away such a chance. I only wish . . .'

She broke off, blushing. The closed, sullen expression had quite gone. The colour in her face, the animation, and the soft lustre in those astonishing eyes gave a hint of what she might become when she was a little older. Martin studied her with growing interest. He knew exactly what it was she wished, and he was beginning to wish the same himself.

# CHAPTER
# FOUR

SIR WILLIAM had told Martin and Giles in advance that the heiresses were to be allowed four days to settle down in their new surroundings before any mention was made of wedding plans. He thought the young women would appreciate this courtesy.

By the afternoon of the fourth day, Martin was feeling very uneasy. He knew his uncle was going to feel extremely indignant at the way his plans had gone awry, and that his indignation would fall hard on everyone, even the most innocent and vulnerable: in other words, Lucy. 'Perhaps,' he thought, 'I ought to make another approach to Bridget myself. Or reason with Giles. Or even give my uncle some sort of warning.'

Yet he was strangely reluctant to do any of these things, and instead took Lucy into the long gallery to examine the set of portraits hanging there of every English king since William the Conqueror. Such sets, copied from portraits in the royal palaces, hung in many country houses, but Lucy had never seen any version of them, though she had read all about the kings in the histories of Hall and Holinshed.

'Henry V is not as handsome as I expected. His nose is too long,' she said regretfully.

And Richard III was not a proper hunchback.

'Giles swears he never had a hump. Or murdered his nephews.'

'What does Giles know of the matter?'

'All the Omberleys were great Yorkists. That's why they lost their estates.'

When they came to Henry VIII, she paused again.

'He looks just as I imagined. How I pity all those poor queens.'

'You may thank your stars,' Martin said, teasing her, 'that you don't have to marry him.'

'It's easy for you to laugh,' she said reproachfully.

'No, by God, it isn't!' he exploded. 'Don't you understand? I have to speak lightly because I dare not tell you the truth.'

'Why not?' she whispered, gazing up at him with those beseeching eyes. She was not angling for praise. She simply wanted to know. She was so very young and confiding.

He took her in his arms and kissed her: little Lucy, fragile and yielding. He felt an extraordinary tenderness, unlike anything he had known before, and was so taken up with his own sensations that he did not hear the door of the gallery open.

'Martin!' thundered Sir William. 'What the devil do you mean by this?'

The muscles in Martin's shoulders literally jumped. He nearly spun round like a schoolboy caught stealing apples. With an effort of will he managed to conceal this sign of guilt, and turned quite slowly, keeping one hand on Lucy's wrist, releasing, but not disclaiming her.

'You are a villain!' exclaimed Sir William, agitated and unusually flushed. 'Is this your notion of honour? To assail the virtue of another man's promised wife, and he your closest friend? I am ashamed to find that a member of my family can behave so disgracefully!'

Martin bit his lip. The scene must have looked very bad, and he was trying to assemble the most pacifying explanation when the words were taken out of his mouth.

'If it please you, Sir William,' said Lucy in a low but surprisingly steady voice. 'I am not Mr Omberley's promised wife. I have given him no promise because he has not asked me, and I do not think he means to. I am sorry if you are angry, but you should not accuse Mr Rydal of being false to his friend.'

Both Martin and his uncle were considerably taken aback by this show of spirit from meek Lucy. Sir William had already noticed Giles's lack of ardour; he must speak to the boy about it. Up to now his attention had been concentrated on the more important marriage, and perhaps he had made his attack from the wrong direction. The person most injured by Martin's philandering was Bridget Montresor.

Changing his tactics, he said to his nephew, 'You yourself are about to be married. You know that is what I wish.'

'Yes, sir,' said Martin instantly. He had taken a vital decision. 'I shall be very willing to fall in with your wishes, provided I can marry Lucy. If she will have me.'

'Oh, Martin!' breathed Lucy. Her eyes were luminous. He had never seen a face so radiant with hope.

'Marry Lucy!' Sir William almost shouted. 'How dare you try to play games with me, sir! You are to marry Mrs Bridget Montresor, and there's an end of it.'

'I must tell you, sir, that Mrs Montresor had declined to consider a marriage between us.'

'I don't believe it. You're lying.'

'I do not lie, sir.'

Martin said this in quite a different voice, cool and contained. Not as a young man speaking to the uncle who had brought him up, but as a gentleman repudiating an injustice. And it was a fact that he always had been exceptionally truthful.

He repeatèd what Bridget had said to him in the wood, and Sir William listened, watching the young couple as they stood side by side. He had thought Lucy a poor little thing, but now he began to see her as a sly schemer with an eye to the main chance. He certainly would not allow her to marry Martin, but the question uppermost in his mind concerned his other ward. What did she mean by refusing the match that he had arranged with such care? That had to be settled at once.

Sir William withdrew, and sent a civil message to Mrs Montresor, requesting her presence in his writing parlour. While he waited for her, he paced up and down in a state of extreme exasperation. Why had these young people behaved so badly, all four of them? In his day a young man would not have dared disobey the commands of his elders, and as for girls doing so, it would have been unthinkable. Bridget was chiefly to blame, he saw that now. She had treated Martin abominably and he had turned to the other wench for consolation. 'I'll make her do as she is told,' he assured himself angrily. 'I am her guardian, and I'll force her to accept the husband I have chosen for her.'

Yet a more reasonable voice at the back of his mind warned him not to take up a position that he could not abandon without making a fool of himself. He knew he would not care to play the tyrant with Bridget; he liked her too much. And she had seemed so ideally suited to become the future mistress of Waldon Harbour, so well versed in all the skills and accomplishments of a country gentlewoman. She had taken so much interest in the management of the estate that the news that she did not wish to marry Martin had come as a shattering blow.

She came quietly in, made Sir William a very pretty curtsy, and said, 'I am sorry to have kept you waiting, sir.'

She smiled at him. He ignored the smile.

'I have a serious matter to discuss with you, madam,' he said, with deliberate formality. 'Pray be seated.'

He ensconced himself behind his table. Bridget knew very well why she had been sent for. She had just had an encounter with an enraptured and almost incoherent Lucy. Once the first astonishment was over, it was clear that Martin had found the girl who would make him the sort of wife he wanted, and that Lucy's troubles would be over, if only Sir William could be talked round. At the moment, he was looking as black as midnight.

'Is it true,' he demanded, 'that you have told my nephew you do not wish to marry him?'

'Perfectly true, sir.'

'Then you have been remarkably remiss, not to say forward, in your behaviour. It is not for young women to say whom they will or will not marry. I am your guardian, and it is your duty to accept the man I have chosen for you.'

'I am sure you would not compel me to marry against my will,' she said in a submissive voice.

'Compel you? Why should that be necessary? What have you against Martin?'

'Nothing at all. I simply do not wish to marry him.'

'Then why the devil did you come here?' Sir William slapped the flat of his hand on the table. Her submissive manner annoyed him, and he was sure she was putting it on.

'I was placed in your care by order of the Court of Wards,' she pointed out.

'I am well aware of it. Yet you can hardly claim to have been a passive victim in this transaction. You asked the Court to remove you from the house of your kinsfolk, because you asserted that they had tried to marry you to a person of inferior station. I have offered you a match that is worthy of your birth and fortune. What have you to complain of?'

'There has been a misunderstanding, sir. It is not of your making, and I am sorry for it. When I applied to the Court, I did not ask them to find me a husband; I merely sued for my livery.'

'What difference does that make?'

Sir William knew what the term meant and was puzzled by its irrelevance. How could an unmarried girl of twenty expect to be given charge of her fortune and let loose to live as she pleased?

'I suppose it was foolish of me,' she admitted grudgingly. 'I had friends who were prepared to take me in—people of reputation. Why could I not live in their house unmolested? I don't want to be married.'

'Good God, what a tangle of cross-purposes,' said Sir William. 'It is most unfortunate. I see now that you never meant to deceive us. But since you are here, can you not change your mind? Martin will make an excellent husband, though I say it. And you will have to marry sooner or later.'

'I cannot see why. There was a time, not so long ago, when many women in this country remained single.'

'That was in the days of the old religion.'

She thought he might be going to add that nuns were the handmaidens of idolatry, but he did not do so. Instead, he gave her a quick, hard look which she recognised. She had seen it before, when she had told other men that she did not intend to marry. It was a sizing-up look, because they were trying to decide what was the matter with her. What freak of piety, prudery or aversion had closed her heart and mind against the desires of the flesh? They never found a satisfactory answer. She did not look like a woman dedicated to perpetual virginity—that was part of her trouble.

Closing her eyes for an instant, she opened them again because the old panic had returned. She had been fighting alone and unprotected for so long. If only she could share her burden with a trusted friend. But that was too great a luxury to hope for.

Sir William had risen and was walking up and down the room again.

'I hoped you would be happy with us,' he was saying. 'You seemed so pleased with everything we showed you.'

He sounded like a hurt little boy, far more hurt than his nephew had been when she sent him packing. Martin had been as cross as two sticks, and small wonder, for she had made herself sufficiently disagreeable, but he had been soon consoled by gentle, admiring Lucy. The older man managed to sound inconsolable. A curious idea crossed her mind.

When he asked rather testily what she had against marriage, she replied, stressing the adjective, 'I don't care for young men, sir.'

'And why not, pray?'

'There are such trifling fellows, most of them. Popinjays. They take such pride in knowing so little. And they change their opinions and their mistresses as often as they change their linen.'

'Now,' she thought, 'he'll either tell me that Martin is a man of quite another stamp, or he'll give me the opening I need.' After a longish silence, he did.

'What of older men? Do you hold them in equal scorn? Would you take a husband of thirty, say? Or forty?'

'Forty is a reasonable age.' She pretended to consider. 'I set no limit in that direction. I would willingly marry a man of your years, Sir William.'

There! She had given him all the encouragement in

her power. She could do no more, not even look at him while he was thinking over this information. She hoped she would not come to regret what she had done. Marriage to Sir William Rydal seemed to offer an escape from her difficulties. She believed him to be a man of sterling character: kind, just and generous. Her maid, Mercy, mixing with the other servants, had been able to find out almost everything that had happened at Waldon Harbour in the last twenty years, so that by now Bridget knew far more about him than he imagined. And he was not so very old. It was his lameness which seemed to age him. No woman need be mortified by a husband who had been wounded in battle.

'So that's what she wants,' Sir William was thinking. 'To become the mistress of Waldon Harbour immediately, instead of marrying Martin and waiting for me to die. And perhaps she has a fancy to be called "your ladyship"; most women like a title.' He was not shocked at finding her so worldly. Her state of mind seemed to him the corollary of her practical common sense, her interest in the management of the estate. She had been brought here to make an arranged marriage, and since she had such a good head on her shoulders, why should she not have some say in the arrangement? However, there was one thing he must make plain before they went any further.

'I have sometimes thought of marrying again,' he said, fiddling with his signet ring. Aware that this was a proof of nervous anxiety, he dropped it on the table. 'Neither of my previous marriages was blessed with children, as I dare say you have heard.'

Bridget made a non-committal murmur.

'I have come to the conclusion,' he went on, 'that perhaps I shall not . . . that God in His wisdom may not grant me the happiness of fathering a family. His ways are mysterious, and it is our duty to accept them.'

'That is very true, sir.'

'You must wish to have children. It is only natural.'

All women wanted children. He did not think the difference in their ages mattered; plenty of widowers married girls thirty years younger than themselves, but it seemed hard to deprive her of the joys of becoming a mother.

Bridget said, 'I should be content to let the future fall out as it may. Whatever happens, I shall not repine.'

'In that case,' said Sir William. 'I am proud to offer you my heart and hand, my dear Bridget, and I shall do all in my power to make you happy.'

He stepped towards her. She stood up, and they embraced gravely, and a little awkwardly.

His skin was dry and his fingers bony at the knuckles. Close to, she could see that his hair was beginning to thin. But he smelt clean, with a faint aroma of tobacco, which she rather liked, and she had always preferred men with beards. She did not think it would cause her any real discomfort to share his bed and to fill his needs as an affectionate wife should.

'So I dare say you think I have taken leave of my senses,' declared Sir William jovially. 'No fool like an old fool, eh?' It was perfectly clear that he did not want his nephew to agree with him.

Martin was too dumbfounded to answer. His imagination gaped at the cold-blooded impudence of Mrs Bridget Montresor, who had come down here to marry *him*, taken a look round, and decided that she could do better by charming his uncle. The match in itself was not unsuitable; even the disparity in age was common enough. It was the revelation of Bridget's character that disturbed him. Would such a brazenly ambitious young woman make a comfortable partner? Would his uncle be laying up trouble for himself in the years ahead, as he grew older and she grew restless? Martin did not know how to say any of this. He hesitated, through kindness rather than cowardice, for he did not wish to give pain, and so by great good luck was saved from saving Sir William at a most unpropitious moment.

'Under these changed circumstances,' he was saying, 'I suppose there is no reason why you should not marry Lucy Barnes. Her birth is inferior and she is not at all what I had in mind for you, but Bridget speaks highly of her, and one woman is often the best judge of another. However, you need not commit yourself unless you are certain.'

'Certain that I want to marry Lucy?' repeated Martin, somewhat dazed. 'That is exactly what I want, I promise you, sir. My mind is made up.'

He had thought they were in for a long and tedious struggle, not yet having had time to work out the consequences of Sir William's proposed marriage to Bridget.

'I am afraid this will mean a change in your prospects,' said his uncle. 'I hope you will not resent the fact.'

'No, sir—I assure you.'

'If Bridget and I are blessed with children, it is essential that you should become independent. Your Lucy's fortune is just enough to sustain you in the character of a gentleman, and I shall let you have one of the manors.'

In his heart of hearts Sir William doubted that he would be able to give Bridget a son. All the same, his taking a young third wife would raise the possibility once again. For the next two or three years at least, Martin's chances of inheriting would look too uncertain to recommend him as a suitable match for any other considerable heiress. He was still entitled to someone a little better born than the Barnes girl, but her dowry was substantial, she was here in the house, and Martin had conceived this odd fancy for her, so it might be as well to let matters take their course.

Uncle and nephew were now able to exchange congratulations, each thinking privately that the other had made a very strange choice.

It was growing late. Martin made his way to the great chamber where he found his aunt's waiting-gentlewoman reading aloud from Foxe's *Book of Martyrs*, while Lady Porter, Bridget, Lucy and several members of the household listened with devout expressions. He sat down quietly near the door and fixed his gaze on Lucy. Apparently she felt this scrutiny through some sixth sense, for she raised her head and threw him a glance of radiant expectancy. Evidently Bridget had passed on the result of her interview with Sir William.

She was sitting next to Lucy, looking complacent, as well she might, thought Martin, though without malice, for he had begun to feel grateful to her. Her pale dress was embroidered with pearls which rippled in the candlelight whenever she moved. He longed for the day when Lucy could shed the chrysalis of her dismal black and wear the beautiful clothes he meant to buy for her.

When the reading was over, Bridget leant forward and engaged Lady Porter in earnest conversation. Taking his cue, Martin went across to Lucy.

'We cannot talk here. Will you come into the next room?'

Lucy shot a nervous glance in the direction of Lady Porter, but she was listening to Bridget, oblivious of the plots that were taking shape around her. She was not going to be at all pleased when her brother told her that he meant to marry again.

With a hand on Lucy's wrist, Martin led her through to

a little antechamber and into a window embrasure, where they could remain hidden by the heavy folds of the arras.

'My uncle has agreed to our betrothal,' he said. 'He is going to marry Bridget himself. Did she tell you?'

'I could scarce believe it.'

'Well, it surprised me too, though I can't complain, since it paves the way to our own wedding far more smoothly than I expected.'

'Oh, I did not mean—I was not thinking of Sir William and Bridget. What I cannot understand, Mr Rydal, is why you should wish to marry me. It is the strangest thing that can ever have come to pass.'

'Is it, my sweet life?' he said, laughing softly. 'Then I'll show you why.'

He kissed her mouth and ran a hand down from her shoulder to the curve of her breasts, small and round under the stuff of her dress. He felt her first uncertain tremor change into a confiding eagerness as she drew closer to him and kissed him back.

'I love you,' he said. 'Now do you believe me?'

'Yes—yes—I love you too,' whispered Lucy.

She did believe him, for she was sure he was too kind and honourable to be merely amusing himself. Yet the whole thing was beyond her comprehension. How could she, plain dull commonplace Lucy Barnes, have captivated this godlike creature? She wondered if he had been drawn to her only because she was so different from Bridget, who had unaccountably refused him, but she had enough sense not to suggest this while Mr Rydal—Martin—was telling her how happy they were going to be.

His uncle would give them a house—quite a small house, not nearly so grand as Waldon Harbour, she was thankful to hear. And she should have her own garden, and a horse well schooled to carry a lady, so that they could ride about the country together and he would show her all his favourite places.

'Would you like that?'

'I should like it above all things, if you will teach me to ride,' said Lucy adoringly.

Martin made her feel that she could overcome all her fears.

They remained in their safe enclosure, Martin caressing her with infinite care, as though he was gentling a young falcon. At the same time he was on the alert, and when he heard sounds of movement in the great chamber he took Lucy back to join the rest of the party, just as Lady Porter was deciding to go to bed.

This was a signal that the other gentlewomen must also retire. Formal good nights were said. Once the ladies had gone, there was still something more Martin had to do.

Giles had not been among the company. He had gone out just after supper. It was important that he should be told the latest plans as soon as possible, and privately. The news that Sir William was about to become Bridget's bridegroom might surprise him into saying something undiplomatic.

Martin took a thin rush light and went along to Giles's chamber to wait for him. It was a longish wait, but he did not mind. He stretched out on the bed and gave himself over to the pleasure of composing a sonnet in honour of his dear young Lucy. He was a gifted poet. He had started writing verse when he was up at Oriel—it was a fashionable pastime. He had plundered other men's pastorals like the rest of the budding Sidneys, and dazzled himself with mythology, yet there had always been a touch of true feeling in his work which made it seem as fresh and new as spring water.

He was interrupted at last by the creak of the door. Giles came in, saw his nocturnal visitor, and stopped.

'What are you doing here? Is anything wrong?'

'Where have you been?'

'At the Saracen's Head. And some other places. Would you believe it, the news has spread, and all the daughters of the game are crying their eyes out at the thought of my approaching nuptials.'

'Then they may dry their tears,' said Martin crisply. 'You will not be obliged to marry Lucy. She is going to marry me instead.'

'In God's name, why?' asked Giles, staring. 'You don't need to sacrifice yourself on my account. That is carrying friendship too far.'

'It is no sacrifice. Just because you are unable to see what a jewel she is, you should not assume that all other men are equally blind.'

'But, my dear fellow, this is absolute moonshine! Sir William will never allow you to throw yourself away on Lucy Barnes. You are intended for the fair Montresor. Or if she continues obdurate, for some other equally exalted lady.'

'That's where you are wrong! Everything is changed. My uncle himself is going to marry Bridget Montresor.'

'I don't believe you!'

It took Martin some time to persuade Giles that he was serious, and when he was finally convinced, he flung himself down on the end of the bed and gave way to an outburst of derisive laughter.

'The old buffoon must be in his dotage to lose his head over that bold-faced siren. And now we know why she turned you down. She was angling for your uncle all along. I suppose she thinks she'll have a son and cut you out. And the other little plotter has done very well for herself. Even if you lose your chief inheritance, Sir William

Rydal's nephew is a much better bargain than I am.'

Martin got to his feet. 'I won't hear you talking in that way. Not about Lucy, at any rate. She is far too innocent to plot. If you must know, we were drawn together when I found her weeping in the garden because you had made it so plain you did not like her. And you have no call to jeer at my uncle. He has a perfect right to marry again if he wishes.'

'I beg your pardon,' said Giles stiffly. 'I am sure you will all be very happy. Only I do not think I shall be here to see you.'

He yawned and began to undo the points of his doublet. Martin looked at him in consternation.

'Giles, I hope you don't think I've stolen a march on you, and cheated you of your promised bride. I was certain you did not want to take a wife, even for the sake of the dowry. You have been saying so ever since the heiresses first appeared on the horizon.'

'Yes, and I meant it. Don't give the matter another thought. I was taken by surprise and I let my tongue run away with me. You know I always do.'

Giles could not have said why the unexpected change of partners had affected him so strongly. He did not want to marry Lucy Barnes, or anyone else. All the same, no one should offer a man a gift and then snatch it away without a scruple. What had shaken him most, perhaps, was the discovery that when it came to the point the Rydals, Martin and Sir William, would serve their own interests without regarding him. It was his own fault. He should not have lingered on here, content with the place of a gentleman servant while all the time accepting, and even expecting, the privileges of a member of the family. It was high time he went out into the world and learnt to stand on his own feet. He gazed round the room he had known so long. Very soon he would know it no more.

# II

## *The Lovers*

# CHAPTER
# FIVE

'THE EARL of Essex has captured Cadiz and sunk the Spanish fleet,' announced Martin, coming into the solar at Wansdown Manor on a summer evening in 1596.

His wife was sitting on the floor, helping Master William Rydal, aged three, to arrange his wooden soldiers. Their younger son Robin lay on his stomach, grunting in his efforts to lever himself up and crawl.

'These are marvellous tidings,' said Lucy, looking up at Martin. 'Did Lord Arcot hear the news from London?'

'From Plymouth. A pinnace arrived there yesterday, ahead of the main fleet, and they sent a messenger to Greenwich, riding post. He changed horses at Idenbrook.'

Martin had been over to visit their most important neighbours on county business. He was dusty from the ride and brought in with him the smell of horses and hot leather. He knelt down beside Lucy, and she turned eagerly to embrace him. Will hugged his father, demanding attention, and little Robin let out a roar of frustration. Push as he would, he only went backwards instead of forwards.

'My poor lamb,' said Lucy, scooping him up with her free arm, and laughing. 'It must be so tedious to be always going the wrong way.'

They were all clinging together, parents and children.

Like birds in a nest, she thought, a nest of affection. The two little boys were remarkably like their father. Martin had hardly changed in the last four years, except to gain a certain maturity which made him handsomer than ever. Lucy had altered out of all knowledge. The uncared-for waif had vanished for ever with her London pallor and the dumb grief which seemed like sullen stupidity. Marriage and childbearing had suited her very well. Her face and body had filled out, her skin glowed, and those beautiful eyes had come into their own.

Presently Will returned to the soldiers and Martin went to sit on a chest by the window. Lucy remained where she was, clasping Robin. The upstairs solar, still keeping its old-fashioned name, was the principal room at Wansdown, where Sir William had established Martin and Lucy on their marriage. The long low room was bright and comfortable, a rose-red arras hung in folds on the walls, and the evening sunlight poured in through small mullioned windows, casting a net of shadows across the rush-strewn floor.

'Tell me about this battle,' she said. 'I hope there were not many slain.'

'The messenger gave no details, except to say that Sir Walter Raleigh was slightly wounded at the start of the engagement. He was the Vice Admiral, you know. We shall have to wait a little to learn the fate of lesser men.'

Lucy knew he was thinking of Giles Omberley, who had left Waldon Harbour shortly before the two marriages. There had been no quarrel. If he disapproved, he had kept his thoughts to himself—unlike Lady Porter, who had spoken her mind pretty freely before going off to live with her son in Kent. For the past few years Giles had divided his time between soldiering in Ireland and hanging about the Court. Once, when they were in

London, he had dined with Martin and spent some
happy hours talking of old times. Lucy had deliberately
kept away, saying that they would get on better without
her. She had no desire to meet him, though when they
heard that he was going to Spain with Essex, she had
hoped for Martin's sake that he would come through
safely.

It was the children's bedtime. Their nurse came in to
fetch them, and they were taken away with the usual
protests. Martin began to wonder whether he should
ride over to Waldon Harbour directly with the news of
the victory, when the point was settled for them.

A servant arrived from the great house with a message
from Lady Rydal. Sir William had suffered a severe
seizure, and would Mr Martin come at once? Martin and
Lucy exchanged a brief glance of comprehension. The
old man's health had been failing for the last six months,
and this was what they had been dreading.

'I'll come with you,' Lucy said. 'I can change my dress
while the horses are being saddled.'

Riding no longer had any terrors for her. She sat her
bay gelding with grace and competence as they rode up
the bare, steep hillside, the actual Wan's Down which
gave its name to the manor and that straggling parish
below. Over the crest of the hill they were in another
world, green and sheltered, descending the wooded
side of the combe towards the golden-grey mansion of
Waldon in the trees.

As soon as they dismounted, passed under the gateway arch and across the inner court, Lucy felt the stone
walls give out a sense of coldness and foreboding. John
Redfern was waiting for them in the screen passage, and
conducted them upstairs to Bridget. She was pale but
composed, her wide skirts crackled stiffly as she turned
to meet them.

'I am so glad you are here,' she said. 'He has asked for you, Martin.'

'What happened?'

'He was crossing the gallery when he suddenly stopped and swayed. Luckily I was there, and caught him as he fell. The men carried him to bed and he came to his senses while we were undressing him, but his pulse is very weak. I have sent for the apothecary.'

She took them through the great chamber into a small ante-room beyond, and opened the door of the principal bedchamber.

'Here is Martin to see you, my dear,' she said in a quiet, calm voice without the false brightness so often inflicted on the sick.

Bridget and Martin went in. Lucy stayed in the doorway. She could see the monumental bed, the carved oak posts as thick as trees, the curtains blazing with birds and flowers in crewel work. Sir William lay propped against a heap of pillows, his face almost grey in contrast to the whiteness of the linen. He managed to raise his hand in a gesture of welcome to his nephew.

Lucy tiptoed back to the great chamber. She did not think Sir William would want to see her at this moment, though he had become quite fond of her when she stopped being frightened of him, and he doted on her two little boys. All the same, she knew she did not matter to him as they and Martin did. She was glad to escape. The sight of that bed always made her feel uncomfortable when she thought of Bridget lying in it with an old man who might have been her father. Beautiful, lively Bridget, who had seemed so independent when they first came here, so determined to remain the mistress of her own fate. For the sake of his great possessions, she had bound herself to a man who could no more give her pleasure than he could give her children.

Martin always said that Bridget had not minded remaining childless. After all, she must have known what to expect. There would be plenty to occupy her in managing the house and the estate. She had been a good wife to Sir William, and her ambitions had not run away with her. It was not in her nature to want to drag her ageing husband frequently to London so that she could cut a dash among the courtiers. Martin thought she was quite content with her lot.

Lucy nearly always agreed with Martin, but in this case she thought he was wrong. She thought that Bridget really had hoped for a child, in spite of the odds against her. She was the kind of woman who would take it for granted that she would succeed where his previous wives had failed. Lucy loved Bridget, who had protected her from the start and taught her how to fill the position of a country gentlewoman. Grateful for this continued feminine support, she alone was conscious of Bridget's occasional withdrawals. Towards the end of both her pregnancies, when she needed her most, her loyal friend had become sharp-tongued and edgy, neglecting to come near her. Lucy had never pointed this out to Martin because she was convinced that poor Bridget was suffering agonies of jealousy. After the children were born she had overcome her resentment and was always kind to them, but Lucy thought it cost her quite an effort. When Sir William died, she would have a great deal of money and no one of her own to love.

It dawned on Lucy that when Sir William died, she and Martin would come to live at Waldon Harbour, and she herself would have to assume the cares and dignity of a great lady. She was not at all anxious to do this, as she was blissfully happy in the snug privacy of Wansdown. Then she reminded herself that Martin would not mind this particular change. He was devoted to his uncle and would grieve for his loss, but coming back to Waldon Harbour would be coming home. And wherever Martin was, she would be safe.

Sir William lived another four days, and Bridget hardly left his side. Kind people kept imploring her to go and lie down, promising to call her the moment she was needed, but she felt that her husband needed her for the whole of the short span that was left to him. Although he slept a great deal, she was sure he was aware of her presence.

Once he broke the silence of a long afternoon to whisper, 'Bridget . . . so beautiful . . . Why did you . . .?'

He was looking straight at her with a puzzled expression.

'What is it you want to know, my dear?'

She leant closer to catch his answer, but he had wandered off once more into the mysterious recesses of a spirit that was almost ready to slip from its outer shell. Sitting beside him, she held his thin, dry hand. She was pretty sure that she knew what he had been trying to ask. At the beginning he had taken it for granted that she was marrying him purely out of ambition, though he had never condemned her for that as Martin and even Lucy, and that conceited young Omberley, had done. During their four years together he had probably revised his ideas and begun to speculate about her real motive. Now she felt she had cheated him. Yet how could she have given him her true reason, when it would have hurt him so much? She continued to hold his hand, while the tears ran down her cheeks: tears of pity and of genuine sadness, for herself as well as for him.

Six hours later, he died.

# CHAPTER
# SIX

SOON AFTER they crossed the border from Devon into
Somerset, Giles Omberley said goodbye to his companions and set a course of his own, still travelling eastward
but bearing a little to the north. His friends were sorry to
see him go. They had shared so many adventures in the
last few weeks: surely he wanted to come on to London
with them, to be treated as a hero and to enjoy the fruits
of victory?

But Giles had made up his mind. Back in the West
Country, he felt the magnetic pull of Waldon Harbour.
And he soon found he was glad to be riding alone, with
only one servant. It was pleasant to experience the space
and silence after being mewed up for so long in a
warship, never able to escape, waking or sleeping, from
the presence of so many other noisy and demanding
mortals. He was aware, however, that his servant Bateman did not share this view. The man was a Londoner,
who wanted to get back to his natural surroundings. He
had been with Giles for several years and was able to
make his feelings plain without saying a word.

To mollify him, Giles began to talk about Waldon,
describing the importance of the Rydal family, their fine
rooms, tribe of servants, rich lands and prosperous
tenantry.

'And flocks of rustic beauties, all reared on milk and
honey. You'll have to mind your manners, though. I

won't have you disgracing me.'

Bateman grinned. 'Are we going to stay at this great mansion, sir?'

'Either there, or at a nearby manor house; I'm not certain which.'

He knew he could have a bed any time at either Waldon or Wansdown; Sir William and Martin had both made this plain. He was not sure how pleased their wives would be to see him. Young Lady Rydal, he thought, might make an uncomfortable hostess for a man who had dared to criticise her, and though nothing had been said during their brief acquaintance, she must know he had despised her for rejecting Martin in favour of his uncle. The other bride had been a meek little thing who couldn't say boo to a goose, so he might do better at Wansdown.

At last they entered the combe on the following afternoon, and Giles felt a quickening of the heart. Memories came thick and fast, and as he made out the shape of the house against the dark trees, he began to imagine details before he could actually see them, so that he overlooked one unexpected sight until it had been visible for several seconds: a black diamond on the front of the gatehouse immediately above the archway. He jerked the reins, and his horse stopped.

'There's been a death,' said Bateman, stating the obvious.

They trotted on, Giles staring up at the painted board with a shield on it to denote the male sex, and the arms of Rydal impaling Montresor. The porter heard the horses, and came out of the gatehouse to meet them.

'If you've come to pay your respects, sir . . . Why, it's Mr Giles!'

'When did my godfather die, Simon?'

'On Tuesday night, sir. Burial's tomorrow.'

'And Mr Martin's here, I take it? No, don't send a message. I'll go and look for him myself.' Giles dismounted, giving his horse into Bateman's care and pointing out the way to the stables. 'Tell them who you are, and they'll make you welcome.'

'I wish I'd been here a week ago,' he thought as he entered the house. That would not have been possible: he'd been on the high seas, but he could have come at any time in the last four years. A stupid pride had kept him away, an ungracious feeling that he owed too much already to the Rydals and would not return until he had made some mark in the world. Now he had, and as far as Sir William was concerned, it was too late.

In the hall he met a servant who told him that Mr Martin was likely to be in the writing parlour. He rapped on the door and went in.

Martin was sitting in his uncle's chair. He gazed at his visitor with an astonishment which Giles found a little quelling until he realised that he himself must look like a stranger. He was as brown as a gipsy from the Spanish sun, and his close-cropped dark beard had been grown since they last met. But it was not simply his changed appearance that Martin found surprising. He jumped to his feet.

'My dear fellow, you come in a sad season! But how did you know?'

'I didn't, until I saw the hatchment. I'm so sorry.'

They embraced as brothers. Giles then noticed that there were two women in the room, and that one of them was the widow. He bowed to her and offered his condolences, saying how much he owed to her husband.

'I thank you, Mr Omberley,' she said in a steady voice. 'I need no reminding of what I have lost, yet every tribute is precious.'

Martin said, 'My uncle lived long enough to hear the

great news from Cadiz. We have all been anxious to know that you were safe.'

Giles wondered vaguely about the third member of the trio. She was sitting by Bridget's chair and had apparently been reading a letter. A very pretty young woman—even at this moment he could not help noticing her subtle colouring and graceful form.

'I need not present you to my wife,' said Martin with a touch of irony, 'since you are already acquainted.'

His wife! Good God, could this be the dismal orphan who had sulked in corners? Giles said hastily that he was very glad to see Mrs Rydal again.

'You are very kind, sir,' said the vision sweetly.

She had wide-set, deep blue eyes which he didn't remember either, and behind the softness of eyes and voice there was a certain astringency, as though she appreciated his discomfort. While he was trying to marshal his wits, Walter Rathbone, the gentleman-usher, came in and addressed him with a deferential flourish.

'By your leave, Sir Giles, your groom is asking if he should stable the horses or whether you mean to ride further today?'

'What's this?' exclaimed Martin. 'Sir Giles! You were knighted in the field—why didn't you tell us?'

'I could scarcely march in and blow my own trumpet.'

Giles reflected that Bateman had blown his trumpet for him very effectively, proud as punch of his master's new importance. Honesty compelled him to add, 'The Lord General created a good many new knights. He is a man who inspires devotion and likes to reward it.'

When they had all congratulated him, he saw that Rathbone was still waiting for an answer. He must make some decision about the horses. Clearly he could not stay at Waldon Harbour with the newly-made widow.

Martin said quickly, 'You will come to us at

Wansdown. That's a settled matter, is it not, my love?'

He glanced at his wife, and so did Giles. Having dismissed her in his mind as a person of no consequence, he now admitted how wrong he had been.

'You will be very welcome, Sir Giles,' said Lucy gravely.

Sir William Rydal lay in state in his open coffin in the great chamber. He looked smaller than he had in life, and younger than either his nephew or his godson could remember him. His neighbours, tenants and servants all paid their last respects, headed by Lord Arcot and his two sons, Charles and Francis Gretton. Refreshment was provided in the great hall for everyone who came, however humble. Bridget received the more important mourners in the matrimonial bedchamber, seated in a chair, but the setting was traditional, the bed being hung with black velvet. She did not attend the burial; that was an entirely masculine occasion which took place after dark: a long procession to the parish church bearing flaming torches and garlands of evergreen to symbolise the immortality of the soul.

The will was read the following day. John Redfern, Sir William's steward and confidential friend, had been given charge of the document, and it was he who broke the seals in the presence of Bridget, Martin, Lucy and Giles. The latter had intended to make himself scarce, but Redfern had hinted to Martin that he ought to be there.

The steward read the opening preamble and started on the disposition of the property. 'I give, devise and bequeath to my beloved wife Bridget for her own use absolutely . . .'

Sir William had been generous to his beloved wife. Besides her jointure, which was fixed by the marriage settlement, he had left her a good deal of property in and around Chelford that had been acquired recently, not part of the original estate, including the former Priory in Peter Street. Redfern went on to read a list of smaller bequests, mourning jewellery and the like, mementoes to friends, sums of money to servants and dependants. When he read out his own name, Redfern's voice shook a little. So far there had been no mention of Martin. It was understood that he was to be the residuary legatee, inheriting everything that was not specifically left to someone else. This, of course, would include the great house itself.

Towards the end of a long catalogue there was a surprise.

'To my godson Giles Omberley I bequeath my manor house of Wansdown and all the land, stock, dwelling-houses and tenements with the manorial rights appertaining thereto . . .'

'But that's our house!' exclaimed Lucy.

There was an uncomfortable pause.

Then John Redfern said gently, 'You will have a fairer house than Wansdown, Mrs Rydal. You will be coming here.'

'Yes,' said Lucy, mortified. 'I'm sorry. Please read on.'

She felt, without needing to see, what Martin had made of her lapse. Rigid with embarrassment, he was trying to stem Giles's astonishment.

'I knew my uncle meant to do something of the sort. I'm glad he chose Wansdown: we shall be near neighbours.'

Lucy hardly heard the rest of the will, the part that concerned her husband and children. She was too busy lamenting her own stupidity. When the reading of the long document was over, Bridget rose and left the room with the dignity of a queen dowager. Giles held open the door for her, then he also withdrew. Redfern hesitated, caught Martin's eye, and followed them.

Martin and Lucy were alone. They faced each other for a moment without speaking.

'How could you?' he said at last. 'How could you be so petty and ill-mannered?'

'The words slipped out. I didn't mean to speak them aloud.'

'Don't be childish, Lucy. You ought to have more self-command.'

She bit her lip. She did not know how to deal with Martin's anger; she was not used to it. He loved her so much, besides being so naturally good-tempered, that she had hardly heard a cross word from him in the last four years. However, he had taught her to be confident, and she no longer retreated into tears at the slightest provocation.

'I'm sorry if I behaved badly,' she said. 'But I wish your uncle had left Giles Omberley any other house.'

'He could hardly do so without diminishing the old Rydal lands. Wansdown is different, it used to belong to the monks at Charltonbury Abbey and came to us only in my grandfather's time, as you very well know. And what does it matter who lives there? This is our home now.'

'It may not matter to you,' she replied swiftly. 'You grew up at Waldon Harbour and I suppose you are glad to return. But Wansdown is the house I love, where you took me when we were first married, and where we were happy. Perhaps we shall never be so happy again.'

She knew this was an absurd thing to say, but it woke a response in him, for he relented at once.

'Don't be sad, my dear heart. We'll bring our happiness with us, I promise you. It isn't made of walls and ceilings. We can carry it about with us, like snails in their shells.'

As she laughed, he slipped an arm round her, pushing back her linen cap, so that he could kiss the line where her hair grew away from her forehead.

'You won't mind Giles going to the manor.'

She did not argue, though she did mind, without knowing exactly why. There seemed to her something disturbing about that dark young man with the kindling eyes. Perhaps it was nothing more than a recollection of the misery she had gone through when they first met. She did not want him walking about her rooms at Wansdown, even after she had gone.

Yet when she saw him next she had a change of feeling. She had been home for several hours, and coming down from the solar found him standing at the foot of the stairs, gazing about him with unusual diffidence as though he had no right to be there and thought himself as much of an intruder as she did. Standing several steps above him, she tried to make a formal speech.

'I hope you will live long and happily in this house, Sir Giles. I should not wish you to think, from any careless words of mine, that I . . .'

'That you are averse to my coming here in your place? I should not blame you, madam.'

'Oh no,' she said quickly.

Did he expect her dislike because of the cavalier way he had treated her four years ago? Martin had told her she was being petty, and perhaps he had jumped to the same conclusion.

'I know it sounds foolish, but I was taken by surprise. For the moment, I forgot that we had another house to go to.'

'If you were surprised, I was dumbfounded. I never

dreamed that Sir William would treat me so generously, far beyond my deserts.' Again he looked about him with a kind of wonder, his hand caressing the polished surface of the oak banister. 'At least you may be sure, when you move over the hill, that no newcomer could value this house more than I shall. Until now, I never had so much as a wattle pen or a bee-skep to call my own.'

In the face of such candid simplicity, it was hard to go on resenting the presence of Sir Giles Omberley.

# CHAPTER
# SEVEN

In October Bridget moved into the Priory, which had been standing empty for some time, so that a good many alterations and repairs were necessary. Martin and Lucy implored her to stay at the great house as long as she liked, but she insisted that the work would be done better and quicker if she were there to oversee it. So she took up residence among the masons, plasterers and joiners and soon had them all dancing to her tune.

Martin and Lucy and their children went to the great house, and Lucy soon found she liked living there far more than she had expected. She was no longer afraid of the size and number of the rooms or the swarms of servants. Martin and Bridget between them had been schooling her all this while for the part she would eventually have to play. Often she worked in the garden and the stillroom, and had always been good with her needle. She was able to give orders in a quiet, steady voice, and to conceal her surprise when they were carried out—though of course she knew perfectly well that none of Martin's people would have dared to disobey her.

'And we don't have to eat our dinner in the great hall any longer, sitting on the dais, with the entire household munching away at the trestle tables below and watching us. That terrified me when I first came to Waldon Harbour, and I never could grow accustomed to it,' she told Bridget, adding hastily, 'I hope you are not offended at our changing the old ways and dining privately in the room Sir William had for his writing parlour.'

'Not in the least. Hardly any families eat with their servants in the great hall now. I would have made the change myself, only William hated to break with the past. I hear Martin has engaged a secretary.'

'Yes. A man called Christopher Downey who was up at Oxford with him. He is very clever and composes music. Martin says he needs a patron. I'm sure he will find more work for a secretary than I shall find for Margery Millard. She is so well meaning, but she will follow me about all the time and I cannot think what to do with her.'

Margery was Lucy's waiting-gentlewoman, a luxury she had done very well without until now. It was considered essential that the mistress of Waldon Harbour should have an attendant of gentle birth to wait on her, whether she liked it or not.

Bridget laughed and said, 'You must make her do all the tasks you don't care for yourself. You will soon find her indispensable.'

Giles Omberley had taken himself off to London, but once he heard the manor was vacant, returned and set up house with Bateman and several menservants to look after him. The three new households were now all settled within a space of five miles.

Sir William's nephew did not have to observe as strict a mourning as his widow. All the same, it was natural that the first Christmas at Waldon Harbour should be somewhat muted, with celebrations for the inmates and tenantry alone and none of the usual elaborate performance of keeping open house for the local gentry.

Towards the end of the Twelve Days, Martin and Lucy rode over to Lord Arcot's great new mansion to join in the festivities there. Idenbrook was the house the Gretton family had built to glorify their fairly recent peerage. It was immensely tall and high, open on all sides, with none of the inward-looking intimacy of Waldon Harbour, built round its hollow square.

'I know it's very fine, but I shouldn't care to live in such a house,' Lucy confided to Martin, as they approached across a chessboard of roads and meadows and orchards. The ground had been levelled and everything was visible at once. As with the house, size and quantity seemed to be all-important.

'I admired this place immoderately when I was a boy, and infuriated my uncle by singing its praises. I think he was afraid I should tear down Waldon Harbour as soon as he was dead and put a glass palace like this in its place.' Martin gazed up at the three tiers of windows glittering in the winter sunlight. 'But you are right, and so was he. Waldon is better to live in. This was made for show.'

Lord Arcot and his family were graciously hospitable, taking it for granted that their house must be the envy of all beholders. They had a large number of guests, many of whom seldom met, for in this part of England where so much space was needed for grazing sheep, most of the landed gentry lived some distance from their neighbours of equal rank, while a country of hills and combes, all up and down, made all journeys seem longer.

The Rydals were pleased to be among so many friends. Lucy had soon been accepted as Martin's wife. She had been so young, so anxious to please, and although she did not know it, Sir William had carefully exaggerated the size of her fortune, so that her obscure birth was overlooked. Now she talked and behaved and dressed like all the other ladies, and no one could have noticed any difference.

'Martin will have his hands full at present,' said Lord Arcot, leading her through a dignified pavane at the opening of the Twelfth Night revels. 'There is always much to be done on a great estate. We have begun digging a coal pit at Hadstow. Have you any coal on your land?'

'I think not, my lord. There are the lead mines.'

Lord Arcot did not want to hear about their lead mines but to talk about his own coal, and when Lucy had listened attentively, he said approvingly, 'I can see you will be a great help to Martin. You have had an excellent example in your aunt.'

Lucy agreed, though she always found it difficult to recognise Bridget under this description.

'Sir William could not have had a more loyal or devoted wife,' continued Arcot. 'And when her season of mourning is over, she will have no lack of younger suitors for her hand.'

He glanced instinctively towards his second son. Francis Gretton was an affected young man, drenched in scent and wearing the padded sleeves and pinched waist of a courtier. Lucy thought Bridget would make mincemeat of him. So long as she remained a widow, no man could exert any authority over her.

They were dancing in the long gallery of this very tall house, a room of such length that there were four fireplaces. The blazing logs threw out more light than the needle-point flames of the tapers. As the couples passed through each golden half-circle of firelight, they were suddenly illuminated. Lucy caught sight of Giles, splendid in a doublet of amber silk, with a chain of heavy gold links across his shoulders. His partner was a bold-looking girl who was throwing invitations to him with every movement of her face and body, but as he gazed over her head he caught Lucy's eye and smiled.

Lucy was slender and remote in her pale dress, the wired lace of her ruff opening round her throat like the petals of a flower, and all his hopeful partner's wiles were wasted.

The Twelfth Night cake was brought in. All the guests received a slice and there was the traditional hunt for the hidden beans. Two of them had been inserted in the cake, and whoever found them became the king and queen of the feast. This was supposed to be a matter of chance, but the lucky slices were generally manoeuvred into the right hands. This evening the Twelfth Night queen was Penelope Gretton, Lord Arcot's grand-daughter, not quite thirteen, and her king was the fifteen-year-old boy to whom she had just been betrothed.

Paper crowns were set on their heads and they were enthroned under the high canopy at the end of the gallery, where they sat shyly holding hands. They hardly knew each other as yet, but they would grow up together, for the boy was to remain at Idenbrook as a member of the household.

'How fortunate they are,' remarked Lucy. 'They will not have to marry as strangers.'

The person she said this to turned out to be Giles, who had come to stand beside her. She immediately felt the awkwardness of her words.

'You married a stranger very successfully,' he pointed out. 'I don't know what you have to complain of.'

They eyed each other with a latent hostility, and each felt the smart of an old grudge. He thought, 'She was a cunning little piece, even at fifteen. For how else did she contrive to put me off with a mask of dull indifference, while ensnaring the eligible Martin with soft glances from those remarkably beautiful eyes?' She thought, 'How heartless he was, at a time when I needed kindness so badly.' And each had a wicked desire to make the other fall a little in love, but only a little.

If she could be taught to recognise what she had lost—if he could be made to admire what he had despised—how satisfying such a revenge would be.

The house musicians had struck up another tune. Giles looked at her with his most charming smile.

'Will it please you to dance, madam?'

She laid her hand on his arm and gazed back at him with a glowing sweetness she generally reserved for Martin.

The dance was a volta, which soon had the couples spinning like tops. The men placed their hands on their partners' hips and swung them round, lifting them bodily into the air. The women had to jump at exactly the right moment, so that they seemed almost weightless. Lucy found that the pressure of Giles's hands on her body, even with the farthingale hoop between them, brought her a curious excitement. When the music ceased, they were both a little breathless.

The gallery had become unbearably hot and noisy.

'We need the refreshment of a little cool air,' said Giles, taking her through the door which gave on to the stairs.

The wide stone staircase ran down through the house like a great river. Archways on either side led into series of rooms which stood empty and silent, and Giles conducted Lucy into one of these. She did not protest: she was amused and intrigued, quite certain that she could handle the situation. She knew strangely little about the art of dalliance.

Her transparent virtue, her affection for Martin, and even more perhaps his deep and protecting affection for her, had convinced the local predators that she was out of their reach. Giles, however, saw her as the insinuating schemer who had deliberately set out to captivate a rich man's heir. The fact that she was ready to leave the dancers and slip away with him in search of seclusion convinced him that she was no innocent. How far would she go in the pursuit of pleasure? It would be interesting to find out.

They passed through two rooms into a third. All were unlit, but the clear, frosty moonlight, pouring through the window, outlined certain dark shapes against the silvery walls.

'This is a bedchamber!' exclaimed Lucy.

'What else would you expect, my dear?' murmured Giles, taking her firmly by the shoulders and bending to kiss her on the mouth.

Lucy struggled and tried to push him away. What she had actually expected was a prologue of compliments and an attempted verbal seduction, which she had meant to repel with exquisite disdain. It had never entered her head that a gentleman of Sir Giles Omberley's quality would seize on her without so much as a by your leave, and start mauling her about as though she was a common tavern wench.

'Let me go!' she demanded, twisting her head away.

'But he pulled her round and kissed her again, forcing her lips apart and pressing her so hard that her stay-busk seemed to cut into her breast like a knife.

When he did slacken his hold a little, it was only to say, 'Shall we continue this transaction on the bed?'

'No, we shall not!' she retorted, and kicked him so hard on the shins that he was surprised into letting go of her.

She made a desperate rush for the door. Unluckily he was quicker than she was and got there first. He stood with his feet apart, blocking her escape and watching her, the moonlight shining on his dark face and his very white teeth, so that she saw him as some sort of wild animal.

'Let me pass, Sir Giles,' she said in a calm voice concealing fear, which she might have used to a savage dog.

'Not yet, sweetheart. It would be a tame end to our adventure. I like a woman who sells her honour dear. It adds a spice to the final conquest.'

This was nothing more than play-acting. Giles was amusing himself at her expense. If she had been a little less uneasy, she might have guessed, and it would have made her angrier than ever. As it was, she was growing frightened.

'I—I won't have anything to do with you.'

'Bravo, Lucrece!'

'If you touch me again, I shall scream!'

'What, and start a scandal? Not you, my little whited sepulchre.'

The horrifying idea of a public scene made her shudder inwardly. 'If you choose to keep me here a prisoner, I can't stop you, but I have given you no reason to insult me so shamefully.'

'Have you not? A woman who acts as rashly as you have done this evening is either a wanton or an accomplished tease. I did not bring you here against your will, and your readiness to come with me speaks for itself.'

Lucy stared at him in dismay. She was certainly not a wanton, and surely he must soon be convinced of this, but the second part of his accusation hit her like a blow. Though she was so inexperienced, she had learnt a good deal of the ways of the world from Martin, and he had told her what men thought of women who deliberately stirred desires they had no intention of gratifying. If he had mistaken her for one of these harpies, she could understand his contempt.

'I'm afraid I have misled you,' she said. 'I don't have what you call adventures. I never went apart with a man into a deserted chamber until tonight, and that was only because . . .'

'Go on,' he said, when she hesitated.

'Because I wanted to pay you out.'

She stepped back defensively, found she had come up against the edge of the bed, and sat down.

'You rejected me so carelessly when we first met, at a time when a little kindness would have gone a long way with me.'

'That's nonsense,' he broke in. 'It was you who had set your heart on marrying Martin. From the day of your arrival. Come, admit it.'

'You must be mad!' She sounded so genuinely astonished that he could hardly fail to believe her. 'How could you think I was capable of plotting to catch a husband so far out of my stars? Or any husband, come to that? I was fifteen years old, terrified out of my wits, and crying for my dead father. He was the only man I wanted. To begin with, Martin simply took notice of me because he saw how unhappy I was and tried to comfort me. A thing you never sought to do.'

'I did not understand you were still so much affected by your father's death,' said Giles slowly.

He must have been told at the time that she had been very recently orphaned. He had not listened because he was annoyed by Sir William's plan to find him a wife he didn't want, and ever since then his view of Lucy had been distorted by the conviction that those two young heiresses had come down to Waldon Harbour determined to make better matches than those assigned to them. Now he knew he had been wrong, at least as far as Lucy was concerned.

'I'm sorry,' he said. 'I was an unfeeling brute. Will you forgive me?'

'That is all in the past. There is nothing to forgive.'

He came across to the bed, took her hand and raised it to his lips. When she did not flinch or turn away, he sat down beside her.

'Then will you extend your charity and forgive my barbarous conduct this evening? I should never have plagued you so, had I guessed what you were about. Dear Lucy, will you promise never to try settling scores in such a dangerous fashion?'

'I see now that it was foolish of me,' she whispered.

He leant across and kissed her again with a lingering gentleness. This time she did not try to stop him. The terrible truth was that she enjoyed it. Then she came to her senses.

'Sir Giles, we ought not to! This is very wrong.'

He let her go at once, looking her over carefully, and helped to adjust the flower-petal ruff which had become rather crushed.

'I suppose I must take you back to the revels. But you may rest content. You've had your revenge!'

She thought it best not to enquire what he meant.

On the way to the long gallery, she seemed to float as though her feet had no contact with the ground. The mists of unreality began to dissolve only as she wondered anxiously how many people had noticed their absence. But the Twelfth Night jollifications were by now so fast and furious that no one had missed them.

Back at Waldon Harbour, Lucy could not stop thinking of Giles, playing that scene in the moonlit bedroom over and over in her mind, trying to disentangle so many

different emotions, and wondering what she would feel
next time they met. Discomfort or shame or even a
prosaic disillusion?

She did not have long to wait. He came to dinner
several days later, and afterwards sat in the great chamber with her and Martin and several of the gently born
servants who were their daily companions: Mr Redfern,
Margery Millard, Walter Rathbone, and Christopher
Downey. This young man had been composing music for
several of Martin's poems, and had just finished a four-
part setting which they meant to try out. He had copied
the parts and handed them to Martin, Lucy and
Margery. The fourth, which he would have kept himself,
he offered to the guest. Giles made a slight demur, but
took the paper and quickly studied the lines.

Sight-reading as a matter of course, they all began to
sing. The poem was addressed to Lucy and was a play on
the word 'light' in its various meanings. She was Martin's
guiding light in her constancy and brilliance, the lightness of her touch soothed away the sufferer's pain. It was
a charmingly extravagant game with words. The singers'
voices travelled upwards in a soaring purity. Only
one sort of lightness was denied to the heroine of this
delicious madrigal, and that was contained in the last
couplet:

> . . . Since Honour lives eternal in your sight,
> Your love is sworn, nor ever can be light.

Lucy caught Giles's eye, and looked away in a state of
wild confusion. At this ill-starred moment, and with
her husband's lovely tribute ringing in her ears, she
discovered that she was falling in love with his friend.

It was so unjust, she raged inwardly. She had never
meant this to happen, and it was unlike anything that

had happened before, which made it worse. But then she had been so very young when she married, so grateful to Martin. He had filled the place left by her father's death—not that she had ever thought of him as deputising for her father, she told herself hurriedly; she had simply accepted her good fortune in a remarkably childish way, it seemed to her now. And life had run so smoothly that her feelings had never been put to the test.

What she felt for Giles was so contradictory and disturbing that all her happy serenity had been destroyed. Being in his company was almost as painful as being without him, jumping when his name was mentioned and haunted by an image that floated in her mind and came between her and the pleasures of every day. She saw that strong clever face—how could she once have thought him ugly?—and the keen light in his dark eyes, challenging or mocking, she was never certain which. Instinct told her to keep out of his way, but how could she, when he was forever at Waldon Harbour on some pretext or other?

'You'd think he lived here,' Lucy said to her husband.

'So he did for many years, and I'm glad to have him back. I've missed him. You don't mind, do you, my sweet? I thought you'd overcome your dislike of him.'

'Oh yes! I like him very well. Only it seems so strange, as though he had no home of his own.'

'I think he's lonely at Wansdown. It would be a very good plan if we could marry him to Bridget.'

They were in the small corner room that Martin now used as a study, and he was perched on the corner of the table, sharpening a quill pen, so that he did not notice his wife's sudden rigidity.

'I don't think that would answer,' she said after a moment. 'They have very little in common.'

'They are hardly acquainted. And I'll tell you how it

is, Lucy: once Bridget has abated her strict mourning, she'll have a great many suitors. There's no one else hereabouts who's likely to please her. She'll never take that popinjay Francis Gretton, and the Bolderstons and their kin are too homespun for her taste. We don't want her bringing in some fellow from outside to become our near neighbour and interfere with matters at Chelford. Much better she should marry Giles. He has one great advantage to offer in exchange for her wealth: he can make her Lady Omberley. She will not have to step down in rank.'

Lucy found no comfort in the thought that if Giles got married he would stop coming every day to Waldon Harbour. Yet while he did come, she felt herself in constant danger.

'You are avoiding me,' he said one morning, heading her off in the screen passage as she came downstairs dressed for riding.

'No, I assure you, Sir Giles. Why should I?'

'I don't know why you should, but I think I know why you do.' He came a little closer, and she looked round nervously in case there was anyone listening. 'Because I behaved ill at Idenbrook, you think I am a black-hearted villain with designs on your virtue. I promise you it is not so. Our encounter there was due to a misunderstanding on both sides: I thought you were a wicked little tormentor who needed to be taught a lesson. Now I know you better, I shall conduct myself like a gentleman.'

His eyes sparkled as he made this rather ambiguous statement, but he added, quite seriously, 'Don't be afraid of me; I am not laying snares for your innocence. You can trust me as you would trust yourself.'

She did not trust herself, yet how could she say so? It was perfectly in order for a married lady to be on easy terms with one of her husband's friends, to sing or play chess or sit conversing with him when no one else was by. If Giles, like Martin, had been skilled in writing verses, he could have addressed them to her. Such gallantry was permissible, provided it was all pretence, and if that was all he wanted she longed to agree, but was afraid she would not be able to hide the unruly desires she was trying so hard to suppress. Once he guessed the truth, where would they be? She did not think she could trust his good intentions then.

As she hesitated, he said, 'I see you are going out. Where are you bound for?'

'To High Barton, over on the Ridgeway. I want to find out how Tom Allen's boy goes on. He cut his foot sawing wood, and it hasn't healed as it should.'

'Then may I escort you?'

'Yes, if you choose.'

She was struck with the thought that riding with him would be different. They would both be on horseback, out in the open, within sight of her attendant groom if not within earshot, and it was far too cold at this season to dismount for dangerous spells of dalliance in sylvan groves.

Riding, they could talk and laugh and spar together and no harm done.

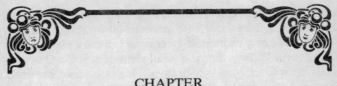

# CHAPTER
# EIGHT

AT THE beginning of February Martin went off to attend
the Assizes at the county town: it was one of his duties as
a newly appointed magistrate. He set out on a Monday,
and Lucy had an engagement to ride with Giles on the
following day. The weather had been fine and mild for
the time of year, but when she woke on Tuesday morning the wind had changed, and it was bitterly cold with a
threat of snow.

Lucy was very disappointed. She sat up in the enormous bed, with Will and Robin scrambling over the quilt
like puppies, wanting to come inside with her and keep
warm. Various household messages were brought in,
mostly concerned with the onslaught of winter. The ice
was an inch thick on the moat that surrounded the
garden, and the milk was frozen in the dairy. There were
gulls pecking for grain in the common field; it was always
a sign of hard weather when the seabirds came so far
inland. It must be snowing already on the hills beyond
the combe.

'Well, it isn't snowing here,' said Lucy. 'Lay out my
riding-habit, if you please, Deborah.'

Her maid looked surprised, and Margery Millard said,
'Surely you don't intend to ride on such a day, madam?'

'Why not? You can stay indoors if you choose,
Margery, and take your exercise in the gallery. I shall go
out while I can.'

Lucy disentangled herself from Will's arms—he seemed to have as many as an octopus—and told him to be a good boy and kind Margery would play with him. In the ordinary way she too would have been glad enough to stay in the gallery, playing shovel-board to keep warm, but love had made her impervious to the climate. She could not bear to miss the chance of meeting Giles.

By the time she had mounted her horse outside the gatehouse, she had indeed begun to have misgivings. Even the short walk across the inner court had chilled her to the bone. Seth, her groom, was inclined to be rebellious, complaining that it was no fit day for horses or Christians. She was not going to take any notice, but then he was seized by a fit of coughing and she realised that he looked wretchedly ill.

'There's no need for you to come with me, Seth. Go back to the stables and tell them to give you something for that cough.'

He protested feebly but was only thankful to give in, and Lucy rode off alone, feeling pleased with herself.

She took the uphill woodland track she knew so well, the direct way between Waldon Harbour and Wansdown Manor. She had promised to meet Giles by a great oak at the top of the wood, but when she arrived, he was not there. She reined in her gelding, Bay Banneret, and waited, slapping her gloved hands together as she tried to get the blood tingling. Her spirits plunged: she felt bereft and a little resentful. Perhaps he wasn't coming. 'Sluggard,' she thought. 'If I can keep a tryst on a cold day, so can he.' But their meetings might not mean as much to him as they did to her. That was the thought that pursued her as she pretended to treat him so light-heartedly.

'I won't go home without seeing him,' she decided.

She could not bear the disappointment, and rode on up the bare hillside. The sky was heavy with yellowish clouds that presaged snow. A few flakes had silently begun to fall around her, but she didn't care, so long as she could reach the top of the hill and see Giles coming towards her.

But when she did ride over the crest, she was caught by a steely wind which took her breath away, and she found herself looking down into a pure white unin- habited world where the snow had been falling for at least two hours. Now she understood why he had not come. He would have assumed that it was snowing on her side of the hill, too, and that she would be staying indoors.

While she was thinking this, Bay Banneret ambled forward into the snow, which took her by surprise until she remembered that he knew this road as well as she did and that he was now practically in sight of his stable —not his present stable at Waldon Harbour, but the one he had occupied for longer at Wansdown.

Well, why not go ahead? They were nearer to Wansdown than Waldon, and Giles would be there at the end of her journey.

She turned up the collar of her cloak. White petals were landing on her shoulders, and on Bannaret's coat as he plodded on down the hill, the snow balling under his feet. It had begun to drift with the pressure of the wind, so that familiar contours were altered. There was a stream running along beside the lane that led to the manor house, and the bank was overhung by a lip of snow, apparently solidified in the freezing air.

This was her undoing, for Banneret, avoiding a fallen branch, moved too far over to the right, his foot broke the deceptive crust, and he sank through emptiness into the stream below.

Lucy was pitched out of the saddle, head first in a flurry of feathery softness. Then she too slid into the stream, just as Banneret was struggling out, kicking snow and ice and mud into her face. She fell back, gasping from the coldness of the water under the shattered ice. She was soaked to the waist and her long skirt was tangled round her legs. It took her some time to clamber up the slippery bank, only to find that he had vanished into the white haze, still making for his old stable.

Lucy trudged after him. Since her ducking in the stream, the coldness of her body was so acute that it felt like burning, and she could have cried from the pain. The snow was blowing directly into her face, so that she could hardly see where she was going, and she stumbled with ever step she took, her waterlogged boots almost too heavy to lift. Instinct told her she must go on. She was hardly capable of thought, alone in this terrifying whiteness.

Until at last a human voice pierced the isolation. 'Lucy! Lu-cy! Where are you?'

'Here—Here!' she called as loud as she could manage.

Presently she saw a solid shape in the dizzying gusts of snow. It turned into Giles, battling towards her, his beard and eyebrows white as though he was an old man.

'Thank God I've found you!' He had to shout above the wind. 'When the horse came in alone, I feared some disaster. Are you hurt?'

'No, just cold and wet.'

He tried to lift her up. She protested that she was too heavy, and in fact their combined weight brought him down too deep into the snow, so they walked with their arms entwined and he half carried her along. Several other figures loomed out of the blur: the rest of the

search party which had come to look for her after the
riderless horse shambled into the yard.

When they reached the house, Giles took her straight
up to the solar, where there was a good fire burning.

'What induced you to come out on such a day?' he
asked in a rough, scolding voice.

'I didn't know—I thought we were to ride. It isn't
snowing in the combe.'

The reason sounded lame enough, and she might as
well have said, 'I wanted so badly to see you.' For she
was sure he guessed, though he merely told her, 'You
must get warm and dry, or you'll catch your death, as my
old nurse used to say. I'll ask Joan to bring you something to wear. It won't be the most glorious apparel, but
she is a neat, clean girl and I don't suppose you'll object.'

Joan was the Wansdown dairymaid. Giles employed
no other female servants. His cooking and cleaning was
done by men, as it was in most houses, and there was no
lady here to be waited on by serving-maids.

Left alone, Lucy got as close to the fire as she could. It
was her wetting in the stream that had made her so
uncomfortable. Her clothes had literally frozen stiff on
her back, and now were beginning to thaw. She had
thrown down her cloak and hat at once and peeled off
her gloves. Her boots were so sodden that she wanted to
get rid of them at once, and her stockings. Her skirt
impeded her, so she pulled that off as well, and then the
bodice of her riding-habit, which was cut like a man's
doublet. Now she could feel the grateful warmth of the
fire on her skin. There was a light rap on the door.

'Come in,' she said, expecting Joan.

So that when Giles entered the solar, he found his
beautiful visitor standing in her shift, her white arms
held out to the blaze, her breast taut under the fine lawn,
her legs and feet bare.

They stared at each other for an instant. Then they ran together on an impulse of ecstatic joy. He held her close, bathing her all over again with melted snow from his own clothes. This time she did not even notice.

'My treasure, my darling,' he murmured between kisses.

'I love you, I love you,' she kept repeating.

Then he let her go, saying, 'Wait a moment. I'll see we aren't disturbed.'

He went out on to the stairs, and she could hear him talking to someone. When he came back and closed the door, he dragged a chest against it so that no one could come in.

'I've told them you are very tired and need to be left in peace.'

There was a carved day-bed under the window. He pushed it close to the fire and placed her on it. Then he too began to undress.

Lucy watched him with no thought in her head but love and longing for what was to happen in the next few minutes. When he lay down with her on the day-bed, his compelling weight and strength seemed to imprison her and then, by a strange alchemy of the senses, to set her free.

A long time later, when she was able to summon the words, she said, 'I didn't mean this to happen.'

'Neither did I. It was a happy accident.'

They had both acted without guile. Numb and shaken after her adventure in the snow, Lucy had forgotten that the dairymaid did not live on the premises and would have to fetch spare garments from her father's cottage. She had taken it for granted that the person who rapped on the door would be Joan. Giles, manlike, had not realised quite how uncomfortable her soaking wet habit must be, or how quickly she would take it off. It was no good saying they should each have been a little more cautious.

'I must be the most depraved creature alive,' she whispered, gazing at him with large, troubled eyes. 'To act so wickedly and—and to enjoy it.'

'No sense in doing this if you don't enjoy it,' he pointed out with a logic that was hard to contradict. Lucy did not even try. She slid back against the cushions.

Eventually Giles did get up and dress. He fetched a blanket and tucked it round Lucy on the day-bed, gently as though she was a baby.

'Now remember: you have been resting here alone ever since I brought you in out of the snow. I'll send Joan up to you and then we can have dinner.'

Joan arrived a few minutes later, a plump, brown-eyed girl, slightly overawed because she did not think her Sunday best jacket and kirtle were good enough for Mrs Rydal. They were made of homespun, a little harsh to the touch but carefully pressed and smelling of laven-der. Lucy was glad to borrow them while her own clothes were being dried.

She dined with Giles in the small downstairs parlour. They were both ravenously hungry. There was a short-age of meat at this season, but still some coneys in the warren, and the cook had produced a rabbit pie. There was cider to drink and a bowl of apples. Giles lived very simply here on his own.

Wansdown apples were always good, thought Lucy, biting into one and realising with a shock that she was in her old home. For the last hour she had hardly known where she was. She stared round the familiar room, which he had altered a good deal. There was a new court cupboard, designed to show off the heavy silver vessels he had brought back from Spain by way of loot from the Cadiz raid. The wall hangings had been replaced by pale oak panels, which she considered unduly plain. The chest under the window, on the other hand, was now covered with an oriental table carpet.

'I've sent one of my men over to the great house,' Giles was saying, 'to let them know you are safe. Otherwise they'll all be out combing the countryside. He's got a strong horse and he'll get there sure enough, but I can't let you make such a journey. You'll have to stay here tonight.'

'Giles, that's impossible! We shall cause a fearful scandal.'

It was bad enough to have betrayed Martin, but at least no one need ever know. If she spent the night in this masculine household, the implication would be only too clear.

'I've thought of that. I've arranged that Joan shall come and sleep in a truckle-bed in your room. That ought to satisfy Martin and protect your reputation.'

She laid down her knife and gazed at him.

'Lost for words, sweetheart?' he asked with his old mocking look.

'How can we make such a pretence? It would be the vilest hypocrisy.'

'On the contrary,' he declared, 'it would be honest good sense. Listen, beloved. You think we have cheated Martin of a property that is rightly his. I've never been able to follow that argument. What have I deprived him of? Not his wife, certainly. I'm not asking you to run away with me, deserting your home and your children. You wouldn't listen to me if I did. And I have no intention of cheapening his honour, that's why I want to make it clear that you are staying here for your own safety, while the snow continues. You have given me the most exceeding joy, my dear heart, but it's not something that can be bought or stolen or locked up in a miser's hoard. Love is like an unfailing spring: as you draw from it, so it is replenished. What you gave me today wasn't taken from Martin, how could it be? He's had all your yesterdays and he'll have your tomorrows, though I hope I shall have some of them too.'

He sat with his elbows on the table, talking forcefully. He was not trying to trick her into an easy compliance. He believed what he said. He could not see that he had injured her, or Martin either. If she had been a young girl, it would have been different. Men were obsessed with virginity, the priceless endowment which a bride must bring to her marriage bed. That was one reason why he himself never meddled with virgins. (The other, more prosaic, was that he found them too insipid.) Lucy was a married woman: in his view she had nothing to lose.

He had not said any of this in the last few weeks because she was pious and inexperienced and he liked her too well to wish to override her tender conscience. Today, however, in his rapturous lovemaking, he had discovered that she was capable of an amorous intensity he had not suspected—and he was pretty sure Martin did not suspect it either, even after four years. Lucy might appear calm and gentle on the surface but her true nature was very different, and surely it would be a pity and a waste to leave so much passion untapped.

So he produced his theory of the unfailing spring, while Lucy listened and thought how clever he was. She had almost lost her critical sense without knowing. She simply wanted to have her actions justified.

Their happiness continued through a day stolen out of time and was strangely topsy-turvy, for after lying in each other's arms through the afternoon, they separated for the night.

Giles had turned out of his own room to instal her there with Joan as her duenna. As it was the best bedchamber in the house, it was naturally the one she

# Mills & Boon

## Love, romance, intrigue...
### all are captured for you by Mills & Boon's top-selling authors.

# Take four exciting books absolutely FREE

TURN OVER THE PAGE FOR DETAILS

Also FREE
— a fashionable canvas bag.

had shared with Martin, where she had conceived and borne both her children. This did cause her many qualms of guilt, and she might have expected to lie awake, tormented by her reviving conscience, anxiety that Giles might make her pregnant (and his child would obviously not be Martin's), or by thoughts of Giles in another room close by. In fact she was so worn out that she fell asleep the moment she got into bed.

There was another fall of snow in the night, and she knew as soon as she woke that she would have to spend another day at Wansdown. She and Giles met again after seven hours of separation and exemplary behaviour, and were able to go on loving and talking in the privacy of the solar.

The baleful snow-clouds had done their worst and gone. The sun was shining in a windless sky, and around midday Giles and Lucy, wrapped up warm, went out to walk on the hard, crisp snow and threw crumbs to the birds that came pecking round them, leaving their footprints like pen strokes on white paper.

They built a snowman which turned into a snow lady with a wide farthingale.

'She looks like the Queen,' said Lucy, pinching out a ruff with her fingers and thumb. So they collected icicles from the water-butt to make a crown, and stood side by side to survey their masterpiece.

'I ought not to be fooling here,' said Giles regretfully. 'My shepherd's up on the hill trying to dig out the sheep, and I should be with him. But first I've got to get you back to Walden Harbour.'

Lucy felt a stab of pain as the real world threatened to break in.

Next morning Giles and some of his men dug a passage through the snowdrift which blocked the lane just above the place where she and Banneret had fallen into the stream. The gelding was lame and would have to stay at Wansdown at present. Giles took Lucy up on the saddle-bow of one of his best horses and they set out for Walden Harbour. They were both rather silent.

'Are we going to meet again?' she asked, nestling close to him.

He had one hand on the reins and the other was clasping hers. It was a difficult quandary. She could not go on visiting him at Wansdown, and though he came frequently to Waldon, he could not run the risk of making love to her there. And for all their self-justifying claims, they both shied away from the prospect of committing adultery in Martin's house. Yet where else could they go? Mossy banks and sylvan shade were all very well in summer, but a snowy February was no time for pastorals.

'I've been thinking that we might use the tithe-barn,' he said. 'It's dry and secluded and no one goes there without my permission. Hardly a palace, I admit, but I reckon we could keep each other warm.'

The tithe-barn was a large building about half a mile from the manor house. Before the Restoration, much of the land on this side of the hill had belonged to the great Benedictine abbey of Charltonbury. Chelford Priory, Bridget's new home, had been another of their possessions, many of which had been acquired by Martin's grandfather after the Dissolution. It was because they had come into the family so recently that Sir William had felt able to leave these properties away from the main estate, one to his widow and the other to his godson. The tithe-barn which stood on Giles's land was unnecessarily large, having been built to store the sacks of grain which the tenants were obliged to pay their landlord the abbot —one-tenth of the harvest. But Giles, the present lord of the manor, was not entitled to these tremendous tithes, and although he used the barn, it was not much visited and would make a safe meeting-place. Lucy began to feel a little more hopeful.

They rode through a narrow passage of tight-packed snow that reached above their heads and gave off wafts of chilled air. Emerging at the far end, they were able to climb over the summit of the hill and drop down into the combe, which had by now had its own share of snow, though without the deep drifts on the Wansdown side.

Lucy was received by her household with great rejoicing, a certain amount of kindly headshaking and reproaches, mostly from Redfern, admiration of her courage and daring from Margery and vociferous envy from Will, who would have liked to fall in a stream and be rescued by Sir Giles. No one seemed to find anything scandalous in her having been snowed up for two nights in the manor house.

Martin was still away, as she had known he would be, and she could not help feeling glad that she did not have to face him immediately. It was hard enough having to say goodbye to Giles with half a dozen people looking on.

She gave him her hand, which he kissed very correctly, and avoided meeting his eye as she thanked him for his kindness and hospitality.

'It was a privilege, madam,' he said easily.

Then he went away and left her.

# CHAPTER
# NINE

'THE COURTHOUSE was colder than charity,' said Martin. 'The judge was in a hanging humour, and we had a damnable ride both ways.'

He had just arrived home, and was thawing out in the small room overlooking the garden which had now become his study. Lucy was kneeling on the hearth, looking after the jug of mulled claret which she had been keeping warm among the ashes. She poured the steaming wine into a silver cup and handed it to him.

'Thank you, dear heart,' he said. 'You've had no trouble here with the snow?'

'No, we came off lightly. Though I'm afraid I—I did something very stupid the day it began, and I had better tell you about it before anyone else does. I hope you won't be angry.'

She was acutely nervous. This was the moment when she had to wend her way between truth and falsehood.

'My dear Lucy, this sounds very grave! Do put me out of my suspense.'

He was smiling, not prepared to be in the least angry, though when he heard of her adventures in the snow he was certainly startled, and puzzled as well.

'What possessed you to ride on such a day, and alone?'

She had rehearsed her answer to this question. 'I wanted to see what was happening on the other side of the hill. You know your uncle used to say we lived in different climates. And by the time it began to snow so hard I was nearer Wansdown than Waldon, so I thought I had better keep on. I never expected to fall in the stream. It was lucky that Banneret headed for his own stable, for then Giles and the men came out to look for me. He decided that I must stay at the manor. I did tell him that I ought to return, but he insisted that it was too dangerous.'

'Well, I'm glad to hear that Giles has more sense than you have. Ride back in the teeth of a storm—it would have been madness! I hope he made you tolerably comfortable. Where did you sleep?'

This was asked without a trace of suspicion. They had lived at the manor house and he knew every room; naturally he was interested.

Lucy felt herself blushing. She bent over the fire and stirred the wine in the pewter jug.

'He gave me our old bedchamber and he arranged for Joan to share it with me.'

'He did what?'

'He asked Joan, the dairymaid, to come into the house and sleep in a truckle-bed in my chamber.'

Martin gave a shout of laughter. 'By all that's wonderful! You must have made a deep impression on him. Who would have guessed that Giles could be so uncommonly discreet!'

'I don't know what there is to laugh at,' said Lucy stiffly.

'You don't know him as well as I do.'

Lucy felt that she knew him a great deal better, and Martin's boisterous amusement jarred. She had been suffering from guilt and anxiety ever since she got home, knowing herself in the wrong, whatever Giles might say. Now it turned out that Martin was going to treat the whole episode as a comedy, complacently unaware of the strong temptation that would have threatened them both, whether they gave way to it or not. If he could be so contentedly blind, could Giles be right that it really did not signify what they did behind his back?

'Well, it's good to be home,' he was saying. 'Let's go early to bed. I've missed you.'

Lucy felt a prickle of apprehension. Once they were in bed together, surely he must notice a change in her and guess what had happened.

She was mistaken. An hour later, inside the tented darkness of their drawn curtains, he took her in his arms, craving warmth as much as anything else, made love briefly but with his usual considerate affection—he was never rough or thoughtless—and fell asleep with his head on her shoulder. Lucy lay staring up into the night. She was only beginning to grasp what was happening to her. She had not felt any reluctance when Martin touched her; she had not ceased to love him. Dear Martin, how could she, when he had always been so good to her and they had lived so serenely together? But Giles had opened the doors of a paradise she had never dreamed of, thinking she had already been to the heart of the garden when she had reached only the outer walls. It was a long time before she was able to sleep.

In the morning Martin rode over to Wansdown to thank Giles for taking such good care of Lucy. They met in the snow-choked lane outside the manor, Giles muffled to the ears and carrying a spade.

'It was nothing,' he said, after hearing Martin's speech of gratitude. 'I was glad to be of use.'

This sounded rather ungracious, and Martin wondered whether he had been irritated by Lucy's arrival at his bachelor establishment, and whether it was her embarrassment which had caused him to summon the obliging dairymaid. He had meant to twit his old friend about this display of propriety, but decided not to. Instead, he glanced at the spade and asked, 'Where are you going?'

'To give my shepherd a hand. Some of our ewes are still buried in a drift.'

'May I come with you?'

Giles was taken aback. 'Surely you have more important matters to attend to? How are your own flocks?'

'Safe and sound. We have no north-facing pastures, remember. I should be glad to help you if I can.'

So he went with Giles to dig out the sheep that were still miraculously alive under the billows of drifted snow and had to be half dragged, half carried to the shelter of the shepherd's hut: heavy bundles of wet and dirty wool with a leg kicking at each corner. It was very hard work. Sir William had brought Giles and Martin up to believe that a gentleman must never be too proud to get his hands dirty. No amount of wealth or learning or courtly graces could exempt them from the common lot of humanity. Serving as an officer in Ireland, Giles had shared the hardships of his men. Martin had never been to the wars, but he could shoe a horse or fell a tree, and his people respected him more, not less, for his skill in husbandry.

'What a good fellow he is,' thought Giles, as they both paused to draw a sharp and painful breath before trudging once more through the snow. How strange that Lucy was not in love with him! She hadn't said so, never would say so—she was too loyal. Giles knew, all the same. Martin had seen the promise of beauty in her when she was hardly more than a child. ('Which I was too stupid to do,' Giles reminded himself.) It was Martin who had cherished her and written poetry about her, yet for some reason he had not been able to translate the full extent of his thoughts and feelings into the physical language which meant so much more than words. It was a pity that he could not be given a hint. But that was clearly impossible.

Once the snow had melted, Giles prepared the tithe-barn for its new role as a temple of love. It was a high building with a wagon roof, sparsely filled with sacks of corn from the champian fields at that end of the parish. In one corner there was a heap of sweet meadow hay which he enclosed by building a wall with some of the corn-sacks. He brought fur rugs and cloaks to make a bed on the hay, and also a charcoal brazier so that the place should be warm enough for comfort. When they were not there, the rugs could be hidden under the hay, and the brazier carefully extinguished, stowed away in a dark corner. There was a massive iron lock on the barn door, and he kept the key himself.

It was not much of a place for a knight to entertain his lady, he thought with wry amusement; Lancelot and Guinevere would have thought poorly of it. But Lucy found it delightful. Giles had the rewarding initiative of an old campaigner, and in their secret meeting-place she could pretend she was sharing with him the conditions of a soldier in the field.

She was irresistibly beautiful, stretched out naked, her body like flawless alabaster against a crimson velvet cloak. 'Venus of the Hay Barn,' he thought, comparing her to the pagan foreign paintings he had seen in some great houses in London. Passion quenched for the time being, they would lie and talk.

'Why were you so frightened,' he asked her once, 'when you first came into the West Country? I can understand your grieving for your father, but what was it that made you so afraid?'

Had it been the size and splendour of Waldon

Harbour, the alarming dignity of Sir William or even the isolation of the countryside, bewildering to a town-bred girl? He did not want to believe that her fears had all been due to his own churlish behaviour.

Lucy considered. 'I think it was the awful sense of being in the power of strangers, carted about like a piece of furniture. Bridget detested it, too, though she was so much braver than I. We'd been chosen by a man we did not know to marry husbands we had never set eyes on, and there was nothing we could do about it.'

Put like that, the system of arranged marriages did sound iniquitous. Giles brooded for a moment. Then suddenly he laughed.

'You did do something, my dear. You turned Sir William's plans upside down, you and Bridget between you. She flatly refused to have Martin, and I believe she offered herself to his uncle in so many words. Your ambitions were a little more modest, but you made your preference perfectly plain. In these two marriages at least, it was the brides who did the choosing.'

Lucy laughed too. Then he saw the tears come into her eyes. He reached out to caress her, putting an end to conversation. He did not want to hear her say, 'If only I had not married Martin.' Martin was there in their lives, and they neither of them wanted to hurt him, let alone hate him.

In fact Lucy's unshed tears were merely an expression of exasperated anger at her own craven stupidity four years ago. What a poor thing she had been, skulking in corners, afraid to say boo to a goose; no wonder Giles had despised her. Even so, she could not bring herself to wish that she had married him instead of Martin, because that would mean obliterating her two children. It might have been just possible to reshape their lives in her mind, so that she could imagine Martin happy and prosperous without her. To think of a world in which Will and Robin did not exist—never could have existed —that was out of the question.

It was no good agonising over the past, she had decided. Or over the present. Even in the penitential season of Lent she felt only a twinge of remorse for the sin of loving Giles. Some time in the future, she supposed, there would have to be a reckoning. She must learn to repent and be sorry. But not now—not yet. She must live from day to day.

The lovers' secret plans ran smoothly, untroubled by disasters. No one suspected them, no one disturbed them at the tithe-barn, no one even commented on Lucy's new taste for solitary rides, which they might well have done but for the precedent set by Bridget, who had always been in the habit of riding out alone when she was the mistress of Waldon Harbour. So Lucy drifted in a state of unreality.

Bridget had now been a widow quite long enough, in the view of most of her neighbours. She had spent the winter altering and refurnishing the old Priory, so that it now made a worthy setting for a knight's widow living alone in proper dignity and state.

She had also started building a row of almshouses in memory of Sir William. They stood on a piece of ground belonging to the Priory and just opposite the house of Thomas Trabb the clothier.

'And Trabb is being as obstructive as he knows how,' she told Lucy. 'Talking of rights of way and pretending that no one may grow vegetables or keep chickens on that land. But I won't have him interfering with my poor old men.' Her eyes sparkled at the thought of a fight.

The almshouses were to contain sixteen tiny cell-like cottages, a dining-hall and a chapel. They absorbed a great deal of her energy, and she was not at all gratified by the number of gentlemen who now began to call on her, trying to distract her from her good works with presents and compliments and all the paraphernalia of courtship.

'Such a waste of time and civility,' she complained, 'when all they care for is the colour of my money. And one cannot send them packing straight away because they won't come to the point.' Even Bridget could not refuse an offer of marriage before it had actually been made!

'I am sure they truly admire you for your own sake, dear Bridget,' said Lucy.

She was sitting in the high, light withdrawing-room at the Priory, and thinking that her friend's vivid good looks and character exactly suited her surroundings. Who but Bridget would dare to place herself in a room with one wall entirely taken up by a huge window, while the other three were adorned with hangings whose blazing brilliance would make most women look insignificant? The hangings told the story of Penelope and the suitors. Lucy had only just grasped their significance.

'You don't mean to follow her example?'

'I don't mean to marry again. Why should I? Now that I have become the mistress of my own fate and fortune, why should I accept any new fetters?'

Lucy could think of several answers, but did not know how to phrase them.

Bridget said shrewdly, 'Martin wants me to marry Giles Omberley, doesn't he?'

Lucy felt herself blushing. Her mind full of her own secret, Bridget was the one person she would have liked to confide in. But Bridget had such odd ideas about men and love that she had not the courage to pour out her story to such a critical judge.

'Is Giles one of your unwanted suitors?' she asked. She knew he was not.

'To give him his due, he has not come near me,' admitted Bridget. 'Either he doesn't like me or he knows I don't like him. It hardly matters which.'

'I cannot see why you don't like him.'

Naturally Lucy did not want Bridget to fall in love with Giles, but she could not bear to think that anyone underrated him.

'His insufferable conceit sets my teeth on edge. They talk of a man being his own worst enemy. To my way of thinking, Sir Giles Omberley is his own best friend.'

Lucy was indignant, but could not say so. Soon afterwards she rose to leave.

'You need not be afraid of what will happen in Chelford when Bridget takes another husband,' she told Martin that evening. 'She is determined not to marry again.'

Martin took this declaration with a pinch of salt. Manlike, he did not believe that any woman who could get herself a husband would rather go without. If only Giles would make an effort in that direction—but his reluctance to marry was a different matter. He was obliged to believe that, though he thought it a great pity.

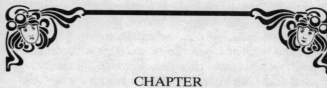

## CHAPTER
## TEN

THE CHELFORD May Fair was held on the common to the east of the town, and everyone for miles around congregated for an orgy of shopping. There were not many permanent shopkeepers in Chelford—a butcher and a baker, an apothecary and a shoemaker, a couple of smiths and, of course, the clothier Thomas Trabb with all the satellite craftsmen for whom the making of cloth provided work: spinners and weavers toiling in their own homes, fullers and dyers. Butter and eggs and other fresh foods were sold at the weekly markets. Small items like needles and ribbons could be got from pedlars, but the other necessities of life were available only at the two annual fairs.

Here on the trampled grass was a circle of booths hastily built of hurdles and trestles and displaying a profusion of knives and brushes, hornbooks, pewter plates, cooking-pots made of iron or copper, bales of linen and lawn and other stuff in hot bright colours, hats, gloves, earthenware crocks, as well as a good deal of tawdry rubbish to tempt the young and foolish.

Jugglers, beggars and ballad-singers competed with the voices of the hucksters crying their wares 'Salt, salt, fine white salt . . . Combs and garters to sell . . . Do ye lack any kitchen stuff?'

Customers of every sort thronged and jostled round the booths, but a path was instantly made for Lucy when she reached the draper's stall she always patronised. Her own clothes, like Martin's, were mostly made from materials they bought on their visits to London. However, she needed coarse linen and kersey to dress the household servants. When she had made her choice, she passed on to the booth she always enjoyed most. Here the goods were not much to look at: desiccated seed-heads and lumpy roots heaped together in shades of earthy brown, but they were the most costly wares on sale at the fair, and the aromatic, nose-tickling scents that rose from the table were as exotic as the spices themselves and the places they came from. Lucy bought ginger, nutmegs, peppercorns and sticks of cinnamon before rejoining Martin.

He and Giles were strolling on the grass, exchanging greetings with their neighbours. A sedate cart bore down on them containing Thomas Trabb, his meek wife, two of his sons with their wives, and his daughter Agnes, the town beauty.

The clothier was effusively respectful to Mr Rydal and Sir Giles Omberley. Could it possibly remain in his memory that he had once tried to empty a chamber-pot on their heads? He spoke to Martin about the alms-houses, more in sorrow than in anger.

'You cannot imagine, sir, the noise and dust we are forced to endure when the masons are at work. And the wagons bringing in the stone have made the road outside my house well-nigh impassable. I have spoken to her ladyship, but nothing has been done. Ladies do not understand such matters.'

Martin thought this lady understood very well and did not care. He made an effort to placate Mr Trabb. Giles was observing Agnes, noting that her flaxen hair still floated on her shoulders, a sign of her prolonged virginity.

When the Trabbs had moved on, he asked, 'Why isn't that girl married? She must be twenty if she's a day.'

'They say she hasn't had a good enough offer. I don't know if it's her vanity that is so hard to satisfy or her father's puffed-up ambition. Both, I dare say.'

Lucy saw that Agnes, dragging a little behind her family, had turned to steal a backward glance at Martin and Giles. She was a silly, empty-headed girl with delusions about her own superiority which made her something of a laughing-stock, but Lucy always saw her with an odd kind of gratitude. If it hadn't been for Agnes, she herself might never have been brought into the West Country to a life so different from anything she could have expected—for of course she had heard the story of the ill-judged serenade which had prompted Sir William to import suitable brides for his nephew and his godson.

'Here comes the Prioress!' remarked Giles.

Bridget was sweeping across the grass, attended by her waiting-gentlewoman, her steward and a servant carrying two baskets. Although she was no longer in deep mourning, she still wore a black dress with touches of white at the wrists and throat and the traditional widow's cap which came down in a point on her forehead. There was a burnish of health and vitality about her, just enough subdued by the muted colours to render her a little remote. With this combined effect of sobriety and self-sufficiency, she might indeed have been the head of a religious house, if such places had still existed in England.

She spoke to nearly everyone she met, and was presently accosted by Mr Peter Bolderston, who had been lying in wait for her. The Bolderstons were a prolific family of local gentry whose ramifications spread into nearly all the manor houses round Chelford which did not belong to the Rydals. A widower of forty, Peter Bolderston was the most persistent of Bridget's suitors. He was worthy, reliable and deadly dull.

Assuming an air of patient interest, and listening with half an ear while he prosed on, Bridget watched a small scene, just out of earshot, which reached her as a piece of dumb show. Lucy was standing beside Martin, who was now talking to the master of the grammar school. Her eyes were fixed on Giles as he walked away from her into the midst of the crowd. A moment later he was back carrying a gingerbread man and a cheap string of coloured beads, which he offered to Lucy with an exaggerated flourish. She received them in the same spirit of mockery. It was perfectly innocent and open for all to see. Why should not Sir Giles offer Mrs Rydal a fairing and a sweetmeat for her little boy? Her husband certainly saw no harm in it.

Yet even at this distance there was something about those two, something in their attitude which sounded an ominous warning in Bridget's mind. A serious intention not quite masked by Omberley's usual rakish air, a soft eagerness about Lucy. She had already begun to wonder if Lucy was growing a little too fond of that black-browed satyr; she was so transparently annoyed when he was criticised. She murmured an excuse to her laborious suitor and left him in mid-sentence.

Martin was now standing between Giles and Lucy, and they were all watching Bridget's progress with amusement.

'What has poor Balderston done that you should leave him standing there disconsolate?' Martin asked as soon as she was close enough. 'I cannot believe that he said anything unfit for you to hear?'

'No. Unless you count it as an insult that he wants to

give me an ambling jennet whose paces are exactly suited to a gentlewoman.'

'Good God!' exclaimed Giles. 'What a dunce the fellow is! The day your ladyship is reduced to riding a jennet, I hope I may be there to see.' Bridget chose to ignore him, and went on talking to Martin.

'I reminded Bolderston that if I wanted to consult anyone over the buying of horses or what I keep in my stables, I should turn first to you.'

Martin said he was flattered. He had some splendid horses and was always trying to improve his breeding stock.

'Tom Stacey has offered to let me have a young stallion in exchange for one of my brood mares. I am going over to Charltonbury on Thursday to make my choice.'

Bridget sensed the wave of interest and complicity that leapt between Giles and Lucy.

'Thursday?' she said. 'And you will stay the night? Then perhaps Lucy can come and keep me company at the Priory?'

'She will be very glad to. Won't you, sweetheart?'

Independent Bridget thought that men who took their wives' agreement for granted were asking for trouble.

Lucy accepted the invitation: she really had no choice. But there was an undertone of reserve in her voice and her mouth drooped a little. 'It's as well I asked her,' thought Bridget. 'She's led a very sheltered life, and Martin is too blind to see the necessity of warning her against that pirate. Left to herself, she would get into deep water.'

Late on Thursday afternoon Giles strolled through Chelford in the direction of the Priory. Rain had been falling most of the day and there were great puddles everywhere, but the sky was now clear. He felt pleased with his scheme for the evening. He had promised Lucy that they were not going to be cheated of their pleasure just because the redoubtable Prioress had demanded her attendance. Now he felt stimulated by an excitement that was not merely erotic. He must not present himself too early, or his plan would miscarry.

He was passing Trabb the clothier's house, and he could fill in time by asking to see some cloth. The shop occupied the rather dark rooms on the ground floor. Thomas Trabb was out and the journeyman in charge, a young man called Jack Summers, was less obliging than he would have been under his master's eye. He fetched the different bales reluctantly, and thumped them down, giving short answers.

'Impudent whelp,' thought Giles, but as he was simply passing the time, he did not care enough to snap out a rebuke.

A small apprentice stood watching for a moment and then disappeared through an alcove at the back. He slipped out into the garden, where Agnes Trabb was wandering about with a dreamy expression, picking a posy of gillyflowers.

'Who do you think's come into the shop, Mrs Agnes?'

'How should I know, Toby? Or care?'

'It's the great knight, Sir Giles Omberley,' said Toby, assuming a military strut. He then put on a dying duck expression, and added, 'All the maids in Chelford would lie down on the ground if they thought he'd cover them.'

'Hold your tongue, you nasty urchin!' exclaimed Agnes, flushing angrily and making a grab at him.

He dodged away and went back into the house to snigger with the other prentices. Agnes stood for a moment while the colour in her cheeks died down.

Then, having made sure that Toby was no longer watching her, she sauntered towards a door in the wall which opened straight on to the street, and was standing on the step contemplating a view of the new almshouses when Giles came out of the shop.

'Good evening, Sir Giles,' she said in her soft voice, dropping him a curtsy.

'Good evening, Mrs Trabb.' He whisked off his hat with the sort of bow he would have made to a real gentlewoman. 'I see you and your flowers have come out to take the air after the rain.'

He glanced down at the velvet-petalled, sweet-smelling gillyflowers in her hand. She would have liked to give them to him, but he replaced his hat and walked on.

While she was still gazing after him, the journeyman came out of the shop and said roughly, 'You've no call to put yourself in the way of that fellow. He's a notorious evil-liver.'

'And you are such a pattern of virtue, Mr High-and-Mighty!' she retorted.

'I never wanted to be aught else,' said the young man miserably. 'It's not my fault I've been driven to sin. When are you going to speak to your father?'

'Jack, I cannot. You know I cannot,' she replied, trembling now, and screwing up the flowers in her hand.

She stepped back into the garden and closed the door between them.

Unaware of the scene he had provoked, Giles had walked up Peter Street and turned in between the high walls of the Priory, to be met by an outbreak of furious barking which came from the stables on his right.

The three women seated in the withdrawing-room heard it too.

'I wonder who that can be,' said Lucy.

She then realised that this was an odd remark to make it someone else's house, and added quickly, 'You have such a good watchdog. I notice he barks only at strangers. But how does he know? He cannot see the gateway from the yard.'

Bridget did not answer at once, and it was her waiting-woman Mrs Laver who said, 'He recognises our voices if we call out to him.'

Bridget had not answered because a sudden idea had struck her, and she was waiting to see if she was right. Lucy had been with her all day. Martin had left her on his way to Charltonbury and they had been kept indoors by the rain. They had been alone most of the time, so Bridget had no excuse for not having raised the subject that was weighing on her mind. She should have warned Lucy how unwise it was to indulge in even the most innocent form of dalliance with an experienced libertine. Yet she dreaded saying anything of the kind. The fact was that she had never exchanged confidences with another living creature, not even as a young girl, and she was afraid to begin. She felt that secrets were the kind of merchandise that could be got only by barter, and she was not prepared to make any revelations of her own.

So here she was, after a day of wasted opportunities, waiting while the servant opened the door and announced, 'Sir Giles Omberley.'

'And what brings you here so late in the day, sir?'

She pretended to be surprised, and so did Lucy, rather unconvincingly.

'You may well ask, madam. It is a strange time to pay a call. I was delayed in setting out from Wansdown, and then my horse cast a shoe on the way. I had to wait when I got to the forge, because Will Smith was off somewhere and could not be found. It will be another hour before

the job is done, so I thought I would take the opportunity of calling on your ladyship, knowing how kind you
always are to the homeless and the unfortunate!' Giles
was looking virile, confident and handsomely dressed:
anything less like a friendless vagrant it would be hard to
imagine.

Bridget laughed and asked him to supper, as of course
he had intended that she should. Even if he and Lucy
had planned this meeting so that they could make
languishing eyes at each other across her table, there was
no great harm done. She would not leave them alone
together.

But their behaviour was exemplary. Giles made himself agreeable to all three women, though Bridget was
the only one who responded with much vivacity. Mrs
Laver knew her place, and Lucy was unexpectedly
silent. Bridget hoped this indicated that her feelings for
Giles were still in the early stages of mute admiration.
The truth was that Lucy was acutely nervous, as she
knew more about Giles's plans for the evening than their
hostess had been able to guess.

At supper, he and Bridget talked about wine.

'I suppose your expedition to Spain has made you an
epicure?'

'Indeed we tasted some wonderful vintages. Unluckily they don't all travel.'

He had finished cutting up his meat, using his own
knife, as was the custom. He cleaned it on a piece of
bread as he went on talking about the Spanish vineyards,
then laid it down beside his plate, instead of returning it
to his belt.

Later, when they were back in the withdrawing-room,
he made a gesture of annoyance.

'My knife—I left it on the table.'

'The servant will bring it,' said Bridget.

But he was already on his way to the eating parlour. He retrieved the knife and then, crossing the hall, made for his real objective: a side door which opened directly on to the one remaining arcade of the old cloister, now an outer wall of the house. The door had a lock and key, but no bolts. Giles had noticed this on a previous visit; he had the kind of memory which recorded pictures in the mind. The door had been locked for the night. He turned the key to unlock it, and went quickly back to join the women.

Mrs Laver retired unobtrusively. The others talked for a little in the candlelight which subdued the striking colours of the tapestry. The room seemed warm and glowing, a contrast to the weather outside, damp and dismal for May. Presently Giles got up to go. His horse must be shod by now. He thanked Bridget for her hospitality, and then, turning to Lucy, 'Good night, Mrs Rydal. I hope we shall meet again before long.'

'Mrs Rydal,' Bridget noted. 'He's overplaying his part.' She was sure she had heard them using Christian names openly in front of Martin. As Sir William's godson, Giles was regarded as almost one of the family. That, of course, was the trouble.

They heard him leave the house, and then there was a long silence. Bridget saw Lucy sitting very straight and tense as though she were listening for something. Bridget listened, too, but all that came to her through the quietness of the evening was the prompting of her own conscience telling her that she ought to make some sort of statement about Giles. Only what? Almost anything she said might drive a rift between her and Lucy, and that would do no good at all.

Eventually Lucy said, 'I'm very tired, Bridget. I did not sleep well last night. Would you mind if I went to bed now?'

Bridget felt a sharp sense of grievance. She was very fond of Lucy and always enjoyed her company. To be honest, she was rather lonely at the Priory. Yet it seemed that Lucy did not care to stay and talk to her, now that the fascinating Giles had gone away. There was nothing to be gained by taking offence, however, so she spoke sympathetically, escorted Lucy to her bed-chamber, sent for her maid and then returned alone to her withdrawing-room, where she sat gazing into the empty fireplace with a sense of flatness and melancholy.

What a fool Lucy was to start looking for amusement outside her marriage when she had everything in the world to make her happy! Granted, there was a magnetic charm about Giles Omberley: she herself had felt it more powerfully this evening than ever before. 'But, after all,' she thought bleakly, 'I never had such another young man to compare him with. Lucy has Martin.' She had often wondered what it was like to be loved by a strong young husband instead of one who was ageing, nearing the end of his powers and pathetically grateful for the privilege of bedding her. Poor William, whom she had made use of so shamefully. She got up and began to walk about, uneasy, not only on account of her painful thoughts but also because she felt there was something amiss, an odd circumstance she had overlooked.

She was still wondering what it could be when she was given the answer. There was a sound of hoofbeats coming in from the road, and the watchdog in the stables started to bark.

That was what she had missed. When Giles left an hour ago, the dog had remained silent, which must mean that he was still somewhere in the house or grounds. 'No, it's impossible,' she told herself. He had reassured the dog by calling out to him, but that would not do. Brutus would not be reassured by an unknown voice; he would bark louder than ever. And she remembered other details. Lucy listening so intently and then wanting to go to bed. Giles leaving his knife behind and fetching it—so that he could open a window, no doubt, or better still unlock the cloister door. Clearest of all, she remembered the quiver of amusement in his voice as he said to Lucy, 'I hope we shall meet again before long.'

Damn them both, they were upstairs at this moment, committing adultery on her second-best bed!

She was so enraged that she was prepared to charge upstairs and confront them straight away, but was distracted by the sound of a man approaching the house on foot and hammering on the front door. This must be the person who had set the dog barking. Whoever he was, she did not want a witness to the scene she was about to have with Giles and Lucy, so she stood quietly in the withdrawing-room, waiting for one of her servants to answer the unexpected visitor's summons. She heard her elderly serving-man come into the hall and enquire cautiously who was there.

Plainly he recognised the voice, for he drew back the bolts, saying, 'Come you in, Mr Martin. I'll tell Lady Rydal you are here.'

'Martin!' thought Bridget, almost petrified with shock. 'What the devil am I to do now?' Dragging her wits together, she hurried into the hall.

'Martin!' she exclaimed in a voice that was both astonished and exceptionally loud. 'My dear Martin! Why are you not at Charltonbury?'

'I never got beyond Farlow. The river's in flood, as I might have guessed it would be after all the rain we've had.' He explained how he had turned back and dined at a tavern on the way home. Reaching Chelford, he had sent his groom on to Waldon Harbour. 'But knowing Lucy was with you here, I thought I might join you.'

'And you are very welcome, Martin,' said Bridget, insincerely.

She had been thinking hard while he talked. Angry as she was with that precious pair upstairs, she was determined to protect them if she could, for Martin's sake as much as their own. Lucy's chamber was at the front of the house, and they must have heard him hammering on the door. Surely illicit lovers, however impassioned, would be alert to unexpected comings and goings? They would want to know who had arrived. That was why she had kept Martin standing in the hall, repeating his name as often and as loudly as possible.

'You will be hungry and thirsty, Martin. Joseph,' she almost bawled at the retreating servant, 'bring meat and wine for Mr Rydal.'

Martin had shed his damp cloak. He looked healthily tired after a day in the saddle and anxious to take his ease. He moved away from Bridget and looked into the withdrawing-room.

'Where is Lucy?'

'Lucy? Oh, she has gone to bed. It is early, but I fancy she felt a little unwell.'

'Why, what ails her?' asked Martin quickly.

Bridget invented some symptoms for Lucy, imaginary but not alarming, while Joseph produced a dish of cold viands and a flagon of wine. Then Martin said he wasn't hungry, as he had dined late. It was clear that all he wanted was to go up to Lucy.

Bridget persuaded him to drink a cup of wine, and took one herself to keep him company. She was not sure how long it would take Giles to dress and remove all signs of his presence from Lucy's bedchamber, or where he would conceal himself when he did. She hoped he would have the sense not to come downstairs and risk meeting them.

'I am glad to have a chance of consulting you,' she said, hoping to delay Martin as long as possible, and she launched into an involved story about a difficulty she was having over the almshouses.

Martin was puzzled. Bridget was not given to consulting him or anyone else. She had behaved oddly ever since he arrived, constantly repeating his name and talking in that loud unnatural voice. Was it possible that she was drunk? Could she have taken to sack and canary as a solace in her widowhood? She was an unaccountable creature, and he thanked God for the hundredth time for letting him escape Sir William's original plan so that he could marry his gentle, sweet and loving Lucy.

Bridget heard herself talking interminably about the almshouses, the rights of the pensioners and the machinations of Thomas Trabb. Martin did his best to listen courteously, but at last he grew so restive that she had to stop.

'I must not keep you any longer,' she said and led the way out of the withdrawing-room and up the oak stairs. It was natural that she should go ahead of him, and therefore that she should carry the taper. She meant to go first into the bedchamber and if necessary blow out the light. She was half-way up the stairs when she heard a metallic click behind her, and realised that Martin was wearing his sword. She felt sick with apprehension. She had reached the top step. The door of the guest-chamber was on their right. Somewhere to the left a board creaked.

Her heart missed a beat. Then she remembered that this could mean nothing to Martin: he could not know who might be moving about in the house.

She rapped on the door, and opened it slightly, saying in a bright, false voice, 'Lucy, my dear—here is Martin come back sooner than we expected!'

Lucy looked out between the bed curtains, her face deathly white in the light of Bridget's candle, her eyes enormous.

'Martin!' she said faintly. 'Has there—has there been an accident?'

'No accident, sweetheart. Simply a flooded river. I was forced to turn back.'

He took her nervousness for anxiety on his account. He sat down beside her, saying how sorry he was to have given her a fright. And what was the matter with his dear girl? She did look somewhat sickly.

Bridget felt obliged to light two more tapers, and cast an eye over the hastily remade bed and the floor around it to make sure that Giles had left nothing incriminating behind him.

Martin was plumping up the pillows and persuading Lucy to lie down again. Her hair fell round her like a silken mantle; her face was hidden.

Bridget said good night, closed the door on them, and went into the ante-room that led to her own chamber. Stretching out her arm in a circular movement, she let the light of the taper run round the walls. Dim as it was, she was just able to make out a slight thickening of the arras near the window.

'You can come out now, Sir Giles,' she said calmly.

The folds of the arras parted, and he stepped out of the shadows.

For a man who had dressed in the dark, he had not made a bad job of it, though the points of his doublet were unlaced, showing the blackwork embroidery of his shirt underneath. She looked into his face, the face of a predatory seducer who had corrupted his friend's wife. He did not meet her gaze. He had an impudent trick of staring people out of countenance, but tonight she had turned the tables on him.

His voice when he spoke was husky and uncertain. 'Is Lucy . . . I hope all is well?'

'If you mean, does Martin suspect her of betraying him, no, he doesn't. Otherwise I should say everything is very far from well.'

'You are angry, and I don't blame you. We've treated you disgracefully and abused your hospitality. It was my fault, not hers. I'm very sorry, Lady Rydal.'

'I must admit I do not care to have my house used as a brothel.'

She enjoyed seeing him flinch. Before he could start making excuses, she said, 'I must get you out of the house. Follow me quietly and don't speak.'

She took him down the stairs, out through the cloister door and as far as the stables. The faithful watchdog gave a warning growl.

She called out softly, 'Quiet, Brutus! Good boy.' He subsided at once.

She turned to her companion. 'Now you can go.'

'Am I allowed to thank you, my lady? I know you've done this for Lucy, not for me. All the same . . .'

'Don't make me any pretty speeches, Sir Giles. There are things to be said, but they are not pretty and this is not the time. You can come and see me tomorrow, after three o'clock.'

By then, she thought, she would have got rid of Martin and Lucy.

# CHAPTER
# ELEVEN

JUST AFTER three the following day, Giles presented
himself at the Priory. Bridget was in the knot garden,
planting out Sweet Williams in the loops and interlacing
of the little box hedges. She straightened up, brushing
the soil off her hands, and conducted him indoors.

Her servants watched with interest, for in the visitor
they saw a suitor their mistress might accept. She could
resign the position of Lady Rydal in order to become
Lady Omberley, and if Sir Giles was looking rather
sombre for a wooer, this showed that he was not such a
wild young gallant as some folk supposed.

Bridget and Giles were both too preoccupied to notice
the speculating glances that followed them. They went
into the withdrawing-room where he had made himself
so charming the night before, and sat stiffly facing each
other.

'There was no trouble?' he asked.

'None. They rode back to Waldon before dinner.'

'I've been on tenterhooks! So afraid she'd give herself
away.'

'Well, she did not. She was somewhat pale and silent,
and Martin was concerned for her health. No doubt you
would have found his solicitude extremely diverting.'

Giles flushed. 'I have taken no pleasure in misleading
Martin, but I can't expect you to believe that.'

'No, I don't think you can. But then I can never

understand how it is that a gentleman who would never cheat his friend at cards or steal his purse can act so dishonourably when it comes to stealing the love of his wife.'

Giles did not answer. Bridget saw the knuckles of his hand whiten as he gripped the arm of his chair. She was not disposed to be merciful.

'I know such amorous adventures are a common practice in London or about the Court, and no one much the worse, but you must have known how different matters would be down here, among a small circle of country neighbours and with so untutored a partner as Lucy. How long did you think you could avoid discovery and an open scandal?'

'Have people begun to talk?' he asked uncomfortably.

'Not in my presence. But they soon will, if they catch Lucy looking at you as I saw her do at the Fair, though I did not guess how far you had progressed. I knew you came here yesterday to gaze at her across my supper-table; it never crossed my mind for some reason that you meant to leave by the front door and then steal back into my house like a thief.'

His face did not change, though she heard his breathing quicken. He was a man who would hate to be worsted by a woman, but he could not afford to quarrel with her. After a brief pause, he asked, 'When did you know I had come back?'

He listened while she explained, and said, 'You are very quick-witted. But I can guess how much you disliked deceiving Martin. I am truly sorry for driving you into such an awkward corner, and for trading on your kindness so shamefully. Will you forgive me?'

'Perhaps. If you will promise me something in return.'

'Willingly.'

'Don't speak too soon. You don't know what it is. I

want you to forgo your intrigue with Lucy, end it once and for all; never make love to her again or meet her privately. It's not for me to judge you.' This time she spoke without irony or malice, conscious of her own limitations. 'I am asking chiefly for her sake, but also for Martin and the children. I don't think you can continue much longer unsuspected, and if once the truth was known, too many people would suffer too much misery. I don't believe that any pair of lovers ought to rate their pleasure at so high a price.'

She half expected him to protest, either by minimising the danger (of course they would be more careful in future) or by declaring that the strength of his deathless passion for Lucy outweighed all other considerations.

Instead he said, very quietly, 'You are right. I know it. I am ready to break off, provided that is what Lucy wishes. It's hardly for me to make the first move. Is she of your opinion?'

'I don't know. We have not discussed the matter.'

'Not discussed it?' He was amazed. 'Surely she must have said something to you this morning, either in gratitude or extenuation?'

'Lucy doesn't know that I kept Martin talking last night so that you could escape. She doesn't know she has anything to be grateful for.'

'I suppose she might not,' he said slowly, discomforted by a sequence of memories. The disturbance of the quiet house, their interrupted lovemaking, curiosity turning to panic when they discovered who had arrived.

'I opened the door a crack, and the first thing I heard was your voice repeating Martin's name very loudly. You knew I was there in the house, so much was clear to me—but I had no time to tell it all to Lucy. The best I could do was run away and leave her. It was horrible. I must have been mad to place her in such danger.'

Bridget was sure that his distress was genuine. Just for a moment she had wondered whether he had fallen in so readily with her suggestion because he was tiring of Lucy and was glad to have a line of retreat. But the misery in his eyes and the remorse in his voice convinced her that this was unjust.

Giles said, 'When you do talk to Lucy, I am sure she will listen. She has a great respect for your judgment.'

'I don't mean to talk to her. That is why I am talking to *you*.'

She looked straight at him, and this time he did not flinch from her glance. Black eyes met hazel eyes, searching and considering.

'I don't understand you, madam. Surely it is your advice she needs? In such a case a woman will turn to another woman as her chief support.'

'That is exactly why I cannot interfere. Ever since we came into the West Country, when she was hardly more than a child, we have been each other's closest friend. By the effect of two marriages, she became my niece. If she ever chose to confide in me, I would give her the counsel I am giving you. So far she has not chosen, and it is easy to guess why. She has not wanted my advice because she knew she would not agree with it. If I force it on her unasked, one of two things will happen. Either she will be persuaded to give up this dangerous game against her inclination and very likely come to hate me, or she'll take no notice, and your clandestine meetings will continue. If that happens, she'll resent my disapproval and be in constant fear of my telling tales.'

Giles was looking even more thoughtful.

'Either way, I'll lose her friendship, and I don't want to do that, not simply for my own sake, but because she might one day come to need me more than she needs you now. If this rash adventure were to ruin her—in plain

words, if Martin turned her out of doors—I am perhaps
the one person who could offer her protection. She has
no kinsfolk of her own, remember.'

Giles had been trying to interrupt.

'I hope . . .' he said, trying to sound confident and not
entirely succeeding, 'I hope you don't imagine that I
should desert her, Lady Rydal.'

'You might not be available,' said Bridget drily. 'He
might kill you first.'

He started to say something, and stopped.

'I can see why you don't want to talk to Lucy,' she
added. 'You are awkwardly placed. You led her astray.
You were the tempter and she the victim, I am sure of
that. Having enjoyed your conquest, you don't wish to
abandon her as though you were afraid of being found
out by her husband.'

He had been staring at the ground. Now he looked up
with a flash of bitter amusement.

'You have an uncommon gift for hitting the nail on the
head. So let me finish your argument for you. It doesn't
matter how poor a figure I cut in Lucy's eyes. In fact, the
worse she thinks of me, the sooner she will come to her
senses and cease to believe she is in love. That's what
you want, isn't it?'

Oddly enough, it was not quite what Bridget wanted.
She certainly hoped that Lucy would get over her ill-
starred passion as quickly as possible, and she had not
thought that Giles's feelings deserved much consideration. She had looked forward to this interview with
distaste, expecting him to be glib and false and shallow
—possibly arrogant as well. A Lancelot or a Tristram,
disdaining the morality of a woman who had never
known the transfiguring guilt and glory of a Guinevere
or an Isolde. In the event, she had found him honest and
serious, and she believed in his contrition. She was not

sure how deeply he cared for Lucy. He certainly cared
enough to shrink from hurting her, and at least he had
not tried to plead his great love as an excuse for behaving
badly.

'I don't want to blacken you in Lucy's eyes and make
her even more wretched,' she said soberly. 'But you are
the stronger character, and I think she will need your
resolution to bring this chapter to a close. Advice from
me, even if I gave it, might not be enough.'

He sat brooding for a moment, then stood up. 'You
have been more merciful than I deserve, Lady Rydal. I
can hardly refuse your terms, even if I wished to. As it is,
you have forced me to face the truth. Lucy and I cannot
go on as we are. The threat of disaster is too great.'

And even if they were never found out, the constant
fear of discovery would act as a corrosive, destroying
their peace of mind and eventually poisoning their love.
He knew that, even though he did not say so.

She began to feel sorry for him.

Giles reined in his horse under the shadow of the great
oak and sat looking down into the combe. At the
golden-grey square of Waldon Harbour enclosing its
inner court, at the fast-running stream and its stone
bridge, the moated garden, the bowling-green and the
cider orchard. He was on his way to see Lucy, and he
disliked the prospect intensely.

He had got to break with her—he had more or less
accepted that even before his interview with Bridget,
though since she was now in the secret he had half hoped
that she would do the job for him, acting as a go-
between: a craven hope that he was rightly ashamed of.

Little as he wanted to part from Lucy, he could have
endured that pain just as he had endured other partings
from other loves. What halted him was the knowledge,

which must never be openly admitted or put into words, that she was going to suffer a greater anguish because she had fallen far more in love with him than he had either wanted or expected. To have inspired such love was enough to make a man vain, but Giles's vanity was at a very low ebb. He cursed himself for being not only a villain but a fool. He ought to have known better.

Martin had married Lucy when she was fifteen years old, with about as much knowledge of life as a kitten whose eyes were not yet open. He had made her happy, and she had assumed that no more rapturous delight existed beyond the affection of their marriage enclosing them like a candle-lit room. 'And I had to draw back the curtains and show her the moon,' thought Giles in a bitter self-disgust. 'Now I must break her heart; be-cause, if I don't, sooner or later we shall be found out and end by breaking Martin's.' It did not help to realise that he minded as much about Martin as he did about Lucy. How could he have deluded himself with specious arguments that he was doing no harm? Their narrow shave at the Priory had brought the truth home to him, and Bridget, a clear-sighted avenging angel, had em-phasised the need to act without delay. He was waiting at the top of the hill only because he wanted to be sure that Martin was out of the way.

He had to call on Lucy at Waldon Harbour; he had left her too suddenly the other night to plan their next meeting at the tithe-barn. Besides, he was thinking uneasily that the tithe-barn was not the right setting for what he had to say. In such complete solitude, Lucy might not try very hard to contain her distress. He would be bound to comfort her, and would probably end by abandoning all his good resolutions. A bout of con-science did not curb a man's desires overnight.

As he was trying to calculate where Martin was likely

to be at that moment, the question was answered for him. The man himself rode round the side of the house from the direction of the stables. He did not take the usual road out of the combe which ran through the village, but came on instead towards the bridge as though he were coming to Wansdown. Giles felt an immediate wish to avoid him. However, he was spared the necessity of running away, for Martin did not cross the bridge after all, but turned to canter along the side of the stream. He must be going to the sawmill, but he would never have had a horse saddled simply to take him that short distance—he would have gone on foot. No doubt he meant to ride on into Chelford after he had finished his business at the mill, and would be gone for two or three hours.

Giles knew he must seize this opportunity. He rode down to Waldon Harbour, enquired for the master of the house, was disappointed to be told he was out, and asked if he might see Mrs Rydal instead.

Lucy was in the kitchen when Giles's message was brought to her. For a moment she felt faint, as though the blood had been squeezed out of her heart so that she was hardly able to stand upright. Then she said, 'Tell Sir Giles I will be with him shortly,' and went on giving her orders to the head cook.

He was a large, muscular man who had come from the cold pastry larder to attend her, bearing a floured rolling-pin in his hand as though it was a ceremonial mace. A maid had just brought in the day's supplies from the dairy: a pail of milk and a crock of butter. Simmering iron pots hung from their cranes over the fire, and half a sheep pouring golden fat frizzled on the spit. The little boy who turned the handle sheltered from the heat behind an old archery target pockmarked from the flight of many arrows. Here in her domestic kingdom Lucy felt safe, but she could not resist the urgent need to see Giles.

She went slowly towards the great hall. She had not yet recovered from the terrible moment at the Priory when Giles had opened the bedchamber door just enough for them to learn that Martin had that moment walked into the house. That night she had been unable to think of anything but her own fear. Then Martin had been so kind and gentle, so totally unsuspicious, that fear had ebbed away, leaving her overcome by guilt. How could she have drifted into such a situation? She had betrayed and deceived him, deadened her conscience to what she was doing, even received the Sacrament at Easter—how could she have been so wicked? One thing was certain: she could not go on living in such a state of sin. The narrowness of her escape—and such an escape—had brought her to her senses. The thought of Martin's nearly walking in to discover her and Giles together created such horrible images that she was only now beginning to understand the iniquity of what she had done.

She would have to tell Giles that she could not go on, though the very idea of parting from him hurt so much that she could hardly bear it.

She found him in the hall being badgered by young Will, who was delighted to see him. Their greetings were public and guarded.

'I was hoping to see Martin.'

'Can I be of any help to you? Will, don't plague Sir Giles: he didn't come here for your amusement.'

'Targe it again, boy,' persisted Will, bobbing round him like a top.

'What's that?' Giles looked down at him. 'Oh, to be sure—you must have your musical tribute.'

He started on a tavern song which he had taught Will

months ago, and which the little boy wanted to hear whenever they met.

> We be soldiers three,
> *(Pardonnez-moi, je vous en prie)*
> Lately come home from the Low Country
> With never a penny of money.

> Charge it again, boy, charge it again,
> *(Pardonnez-moi, je vous en prie)*
> As long as you have any ink in your pen,
> With never a penny of money.

Lucy listened to him chanting the far from romantic words of this low ditty and thought she had never loved him so much. That was the terrible sorcery of love. One man's slightest action seemed to be able to outweigh the whole devotion of anyone else.

Will was removed by his nurse, and Giles said, 'Shall we go out and take the air?'

It was wiser than trying to talk indoors. Waldon Harbour was a warren of adjoining rooms, a place where people overheard conversations even without meaning to.

The enclosed garden hardly seemed safe, either. They passed the gently rippling moat and reached the short turf of the bowling-green. They could be seen from the house, but not heard.

'My dear little love,' he said, 'have you been very much frightened? I can never forgive myself for leading you into such danger!'

'It was my own fault. I should never have agreed.' She spoke hardly above a whisper.

'Well, we need not apportion blame. And we were luckier than we deserved. He doesn't suspect?'

'No. He is far too good and trusting. That makes it worse.'

There was a pause while they were both plucking up their courage.

Then Giles said, 'I don't think we can go on meeting as lovers. There's too much at stake: Martin's happiness, as well as our own; your marriage and your children.'

Lucy bit her lip. These were more or less the words she had meant to say to him, yet when she heard them they were like a death sentence. She realised that she had been expecting that he would refuse to make the break, compel her to go on. His will was stronger than hers, and she could not have withstood him. 'What a hypocrite I am,' she thought, hating herself.

'I'm glad you think as I do.' She forced out the words. 'For I had come to the same conclusion. We can't go on. Yet we can't go back, either, to what we used to be. Oh, why did we ever fall into this trap?'

'Because I was a blind, egotistical fool. I didn't see the danger. I didn't see how this would change everything.'

He felt her hand tremble on his arm and saw that she was silently weeping. They had come to the edge of the bowling-green. He did not want to turn so that her face would be visible to any watcher from a window. Ahead of them lay the cider orchard, a safe enough haven, he thought, for no one would be working here at this season. He led her in among the apple trees. The blossom was beginning to fall as the young fruit set.

'How strange,' thought Lucy. 'On the first day of our love the snow was coming down like petals. Now the petals are coming down like snow.'

There was a twisted old tree, bent almost to the ground. Beneath its friendly boughs they sat on the grass and he comforted her. He was no longer afraid of being aroused by her closeness. The sight of her mute suffering and his own remorse had driven away every other sensation.

So he talked to her gently, saying he had never loved any woman so much before. This was true so far as it went—until now he had prided himself on his cold and well-regulated heart: now he was ashamed of having taken so much and given so little. When the worst pain of parting was over, he suggested, they would be able to look back without regret.

'Never!' burst out Lucy. 'I wish I were dead.'

'My dearest treasure, you mustn't say so! You will soon feel differently, I promise.'

'I may have to live differently, but I shall feel the same for ever.'

# III

*The Adversaries*

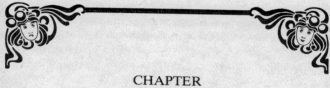

# CHAPTER
# TWELVE

GILES HAD been right in assuming that Martin would not have had a horse saddled simply to go to the sawmill. What he had not known was that Martin had been out on horseback for a couple of hours already, seeing tenants at Higher Waldon, which lay beyond the northern slope of the combe. The trip to the sawmill had come at the end of his ride, not at the beginning.

When he had finished there, he came home, dismounted and went indoors. He was then told of Giles's visit.

'Is he still here?'

'I think so, sir,' said Christopher Downey, the secretary. 'He asked for Mrs Rydal.'

'They went across to the orchard,' volunteered Rathbone, the ever-helpful gentleman-usher.

Martin decided to follow them, happy in the unquestioning certainty that he would be welcome. Probably Giles wanted advice about apple trees or cider-making: he had begun to take a great interest in husbandry since inheriting land of his own.

Martin strolled towards the orchard, soundless on the smooth turf of the bowling-green. As he approached the tight rows of trees he could hear voices, and paused, trying to locate the speakers among the maze of branches. A woman's voice rose, brutally unexpected.

'Never! I wish I were dead.'

It was Lucy, unmistakably Lucy in spite of the choking sobs. Martin stopped, stupidly bewildered, not understanding.

'My dearest treasure, you mustn't say so! You will soon feel differently.' And that voice he had known even longer.

Lucy's reply, heard through a terrible confusion of pain and shock, struck the final blow.

'I may have to live differently, but I shall feel the same for ever.'

Martin heard no more. He turned and fled. Later he would be able to calculate alternatives. Now, as the first terrible comprehension swept over him, he could act only on impulse, and the impulse might just as well have driven him in among the apple trees to confront the two people he had loved and trusted. Perhaps he felt an instinctive need to avoid them because he could not bear the pain. He had to be alone. To think. To convince his dazed and wounded mind that those cruel words actually meant what they appeared to mean.

He could not go back to the house to be talked to and stared at, so he began to climb the steep side of the combe and was soon safely hidden in the woods. He pushed clumsily through the undergrowth, scratching his hands, stumbling over roots.

Presently he fell and simply lay on the ground, pressing his cheek against the damp moss, too wretched to move. His lovely Lucy—how could she have turned away from him? He loved her with all his heart, and he had always believed that she was as happy as he was. Yet he could still hear the intense feeling in her voice as she said, not to him but to Giles, 'I shall feel the same for ever.'

'What am I to do?' he asked aloud, staring up into the canopy of leaves. All the trees were fresh and brilliant in their different shades of green. Later they would grow dark and heavy: now they made a wonderful mosaic of lime and hazel, oak and hornbeam. And the air was full of little singing birds, their notes so sweet that they added to his pain.

'What am I to do?' he asked again.

He looked around him. He was not far from the track which ran over the hill to Wansdown. Presently Giles would come riding back this way. He would stand in his path and accuse him: that would be better than starting a brawl in Lucy's presence. He had only to stay here and wait.

By now, though he did not know it, Giles had already left Waldon Harbour. Unhappy, and haunted by Lucy's even greater unhappiness, he had not been able to face the immediate prospect of going home alone, so he had ridden to Chelford instead. He would leave a message at the Priory to tell Bridget that he had kept his promise, and then perhaps he'd find a companion to drink with him at the Saracen's Head before he returned to Wansdown by the other route.

So Martin sat with his elbows on his knees, plunged in misery and hardly aware of the passage of time, yet gradually able to think more rationally about what he had overheard in the orchard.

They were in love but they were unhappy, preparing to part. What he had come on was a renunciation scene. This did nothing to relieve his despair. If Lucy had ceased to care for him, it hardly mattered what she felt for the man who had supplanted him. He wondered how long he had been unconsciously standing in their way. It was horrible to find oneself an obstacle, the cause, perhaps hated and resented, of the self-denial that was costing Lucy so much. Poor girl, she had such a tender conscience. And Giles had no conscience at all, he thought angrily. He'd been chasing women since he was sixteen. He thought nothing of poaching on other men's preserves; that simply added to the sport.

Yes, Martin could see it all. Giles had set out to fascinate Lucy; he'd never forgotten her indifference five years ago; and the innocent girl had indulged in a little harmless dalliance and lost her heart in the process. His imagination hurried past the nature of the dalliance. He could not endure the suspicion that she had done anything seriously wrong. And if there had been nothing worse than a few kisses, then surely he need not give up hope?

What he had overheard in the orchard had been a momentary cry of desolation, a grief that would soon lose its sharpness. And if this were so, he simply had to be patient and wait for her to recover. Wait, and do nothing rash. Certainly not challenge Giles to a duel. He saw now that his greatest strength lay in pretended ignorance. It would be a difficult part to play, but for Lucy's sake he must manage it.

It was early evening when he returned to the house. Lucy and Margery were in the great chamber, embroidering different ends of a long narrow piece of material that was to make the valance for a bed. At least Margery was embroidering; Lucy was merely picking at the linen with her needle. She had cried so much that she could hardly see what she was doing. Her eyelids were puffy but not red, and her deep unhappiness had made her look sullen, just as the fifteen-year-old Lucy had looked, pining for her dead father.

Margery thought she was cross. She considered her mistress unpredictable, like many great ladies. Martin knew she was miserable.

'You have been gone a long time,' she said to him, anxious and conciliating because she felt so guilty.

'I had much business to attend to.'

He picked up a book and tried to read.

They had several members of the household at supper with them. Afterwards, Martin retreated to his study and sat brooding in the dusk. On his table there was a half-written sonnet which he had begun the day before. He had written so many verses for Lucy, and now their vapid irrelevance taunted him. What sense was there in all those artificial metaphors, star-bright eyes and dove-white breasts? What sort of a fool wasted his time on rhyming couplets while his wife was falling in love with his closest friend?

He dragged himself to bed at last, late enough to hope that Lucy might be asleep. She wasn't, as he knew from the change in her breathing, but she was able to give a fairly good imitation, while he went through the farce of not disturbing her.

Chelford church was dedicated to St Peter, and for many centuries there had been a holiday in the town on the twenty-ninth of June, the citizens attending Mass before the secular festivities. Now these festivities were entirely secular. The principal merchants held a banquet in the market hall and many of the local gentry were invited.

Martin was asked as a matter of course and felt obliged to go, though he was in no mood to enjoy himself. The carefully concealed wretchedness of the past few weeks seemed to drag on him with the weight of a millstone.

He stabled his horse at the Priory, and was surprised to meet Giles coming from the house on foot.

'What are you doing here?' he asked, more sharply than he intended.

'I have been taking her ladyship a tribute of

strawberries. Her own plants are too young to bear this year. Do you object?'

'No, why should I?'

Martin was a little confused. He no longer wanted this arch-deceiver to marry Bridget and gain control of her fortune, but he could hardly say so while keeping up the fiction that nothing was wrong between them. Was Giles now pursuing Bridget? Was this why he had ended his intrigue with Lucy?

They had fallen into step together as they walked. Since they were both bound for the banquet, they could hardly do anything else. Ahead of them were the new almshouses, recently finished and occupied.

Giles said something about Bridget's generosity to the town. 'And she tells me she thinks of enlarging the grammar school.'

'Does she, indeed? She has said nothing to me.'

Martin had an idea that Bridget was inclined to interfere a little too much in the affairs of Chelford, assuming to herself the rights of patronage that had always come direct from Waldon Harbour. In his present state of gloom and irritation, this annoyed him more than it should have done.

'I may have misunderstood her,' said Giles quickly. 'I dare say it was no more than a passing whim.'

'Very likely. She is an odd woman. I arrived at the Priory one evening when she wasn't expecting me—it was the day I tried to go to Charltonbury and had to turn back because the river was in flood. She received me in the most fulsome manner. I could have sworn that she was drunk.'

'Oh, come, my dear fellow, I'm sure you are mistaken. She was perfectly sober at supper.'

Giles felt bound to defend Bridget, knowing only too well that he was responsible for her odd behaviour. In saying he had seen her at suppertime, he did not think he was telling anything new. There was no secret about his having been at the Priory earlier that evening: why should there be? It did not occur to him that both Bridget and Lucy had avoided all mention of his name for fear of sounding guilty and unnatural.

His attention was distracted just then by a friend who came to join them: Humphrey Bolderston, the younger brother of Bridget's earnest suitor.

While they were greeting each other, Martin stood a little apart, mentally reeling. 'She was perfectly sober at supper.' So Giles had supped at the Priory, and they had not told him. He saw their silence as a deliberate conspiracy, and the reason for it flashed through his brain with a merciless clarity. That villain had still been in the house when he got there. Giles had taken the opportunity of spending the night with Lucy while he was away, with Bridget aiding and abetting. That explained her strange antics. She hadn't been drunk: she had been fighting a rearguard action to prevent his catching his wife in the arms of her lover.

Giles and Humphrey Bolderston were moving on. The road was muddy and rutted, and there was not room for three to walk abreast, which was just as well. Martin was able to fall in behind them, still wrestling with his own dark thoughts. What a fool he had been to imagine that Lucy might have lost her heart and remained faithful! She was an adulteress, and he was a cuckold, and what was he going to do about it? He had been knocked stupid by the shock and could not think clearly. He stared at Giles's broad shoulders and straight back, and hated him.

By now they had reached the centre of the town, which was packed with people. All the young men and maidens were dressed in their finery, strolling up and down in groups or in couples. Many were setting off for the woods. Later there would be dancing.

The men of consequence converged on the Market Hall, a rectangular building raised impressively on solid stone pillars. The lower floor, open on all sides, was used as a cool and shady butter-market. There was a crush on the staircase, so Martin had time to collect himself and remember what was expected of him. He was Rydal of Waldon Harbour, the head of the oldest family in the neighbourhood, and no private distress must be allowed to come between him and his public duties.

As he entered the hall he saw the Mayor, Simon Honeycombe, coming towards him. Preparing to play the part of the guest of honour, he was about to step forward when he realised, just in time, that Honeycombe was looking not at him but at Giles, who was now by virtue of his rank the most important person present.

Such a snub, on top of everything else, was unendurable; he was seething with resentment, and this time he could not hide his feelings.

Turning to Humphrey Bolderston, he said contemptuously, 'Our worthy hosts seem much impressed with Omberley's knighthood. I suppose the London estimate of such honours cannot have reached them yet. You've heard the rhyme, I take it?

A knight of Coles, a squire of Wales,
A lord of the North Country,
A yeoman of Kent with his good rent
Can buy them up all three.'

It was well known that the Queen had not been at all pleased by the lavish manner in which the Earl of Essex had bestowed knighthoods after the victory at Cadiz, some of his new knights being hardly more than landless adventurers. Giles might have been one of these but for Sir William's timely bequest, though Martin had never allowed anyone to hint as much in his presence. No wonder Bolderston was eyeing him curiously.

He cursed his own folly. He had managed to hide his deep and well-justified jealousy, only to reveal a petty spite which would make him a laughing-stock.

He was summoned to sit on the Mayor's left, and glumly took his place. The table was weighed down with rich food, so that you could hardly put a finger between the dishes. The hall smelt of meat and game and spice, and of the merchants sweating in their fur-trimmed gowns. Sugar confections began to wilt in the steamy atmosphere, and the town waits set up a great braying and booming of shawms and sackbuts in the gallery overhead.

Martin got through the banquet somehow, hardly knowing what he was eating or saying. When at last it was over and they were released into the fresh air, Giles murmured to him confidentially, 'We have done our duty with conspicuous merit, don't you think? Thank God these junketings happen only once a year.'

It was difficult not to fall into the old ways, to smile and compare incidents of private amusement. As they went to fetch their horses from the Priory, Martin was astonished to hear himself say, 'Why don't you come back to Waldon Harbour with me? We have not seen you there for some time.'

'I should be glad to,' said Giles, after the briefest hesitation.

'What the devil made me ask him,' Martin wondered, immediately regretting his extraordinary impulse. Perhaps he needed to see Giles and Lucy together before he could make up his mind what to do next. The full knowledge of their treachery had come to him in two separate shocks, like repeated blows of the axe in a botched execution. He had lost the impetus of his original rage and felt himself slipping into a terrible indecision.

Host and guest were both rather silent on the ride. Giles did not want to go to Waldon Harbour, where he knew the sight of Lucy would be disturbing, but he had not liked to refuse. He had realised at once that Martin had disliked giving him precedence at the banquet, and was afraid that others had noticed as well. He was sorry to find that Martin should be so paltry, but he was in no position to pass judgment, and it seemed important that everyone should know they were still on the friendliest terms.

They found Lucy in the moated gardens, in one of the leafy bowers, sitting with her hands in her lap, gazing out from the shade at the dizzy patterns in the knot garden. For once in this wet summer the plants looked bright and hot.

'You are pensive, my dear heart,' said Martin, 'and a little melancholy, I think. But I have brought you the right cure.'

He sat down on the stone paving at her feet, leaving it open to Giles to share the bench with her. Giles chose to lean against the wooden palisade which supported the pleached alley. He thought Lucy looked pale in the shade, and that her face had grown thinner.

Martin now became exuberant, talking hard and running from one subject to another. There was a book he wanted Giles to read. He jumped up, saying that he would fetch it at once.

'There is no urgency. You can give it to me later.'

But Martin was already half-way along the little path. As he turned the corner to cross the moat, Giles and

Lucy found themselves alone.

'How goes it, my dear?' he asked in a low voice.

Lucy seemed to find some difficulty in answering, and before she did so they heard a footfall close to them.

Martin was suddenly back with them, saying, 'I can't let you have that book today. I remember that I've lent it to Christopher.'

There was a curious silence.

'It does not signify,' said Giles, thinking, 'He's found out. That was a trap to catch us kissing or fondling. Why else should he go so noisily and come back so quietly and so soon?' He glanced at Lucy to see whether she had grasped the point, but she was gazing into the distance, apparently oblivious.

Martin began his monologue again, discursive and disjointed. He had no idea how badly he was acting. Tormented by jealousy, he was also trying to deal with a difficulty he had not foreseen: the need for a deceived husband to connive at his own deception. If the truth came out openly, he would be forced to make some kind of stand. A gentleman was obliged to defend his honour when it was threatened. Yet he had been taught to think of duelling as a last resort, frowned on by the Queen and the Church, and though he longed to plunge three inches of steel into Giles's heart, he might only be making a bad situation worse. If he fought Giles, he would simply draw attention to a family disgrace which apparently no one else even suspected. There would be a great scandal, and Lucy's ruined reputation would cast a blight on everyone connected with her, including their children.

He had realised all this just as he had set foot on the little bridge across the moat. That was why he had turned back at once, before Giles and Lucy had had time to fall into each other's arms. He would go on pretending ignorance while painfully conscious of the sorry figure he cut, an unprotesting cuckold, the most abject creature on earth. He was quite as anxious to keep their guilty secret as they were.

He went on talking. Giles became restless. Lucy sat like a statue, and presently one of the maids came out from the house to say that Master Robin had the earache and nurse begged that madam would come. The little boy was calling her.

Lucy got up and went indoors. Both men stared after her.

'She is a very good mother,' said Giles.

'Oh yes, she is a good mother.' Martin could not hear the desolation in his own voice.

Giles was by now very uneasy. He stayed on at Waldon Harbour until after supper. He was hoping to have a word alone with Lucy so that he could warn her. He also felt he should remain to answer any accusation that Martin cared to make. But Lucy was shut up with the sick child, and Martin said nothing whatever about his private concerns.

The moon was up by the time Giles rode over the hill to Wansdown. He was very disturbed, and wished fervently that he had never made love to Lucy Rydal.

Unsaddling his horse in the stable, he found his soldier servant Bateman doing the same, as he had also been in Chelford for the Peter's Day revels.

'You're back sooner than I looked for,' Giles rallied him. 'Wasn't your charmer as kind as you hoped?'

'She was willing, sir,' said Batemen confidently. 'But something happened to spoil our evening. A young woman's missing, not seen since midday or thereabouts, and there's been a search-party out looking for her. We gave up only when it grew too dark.'

'Surely on such a day as this there must be plenty of

young women, and young men too, who can't be easily accounted for?'

'That's what I thought at first, sir. But there doesn't seem to be a man in the case, and the wench is that daughter of Trabb the clothier, who's well known to be an icicle. The townsfolk think she must have met with an accident.'

'Agnes Trabb? I'm sorry to hear it. If she hasn't come home by morning, we must join the search.'

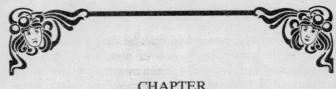

# CHAPTER
# THIRTEEN

THE DISAPPEARANCE of Agnes Trabb was causing a great
deal of wonder and speculation in Chelford. Complaining of a headache on the morning of St Peter's Day, she
had not gone with her mother to help superintend the
arrangements for the banquet. When Mrs Trabb had gone
to the house, she found that Agnes had dressed and gone
out. It was taken for granted that she had recovered and
gone round to one of her married sisters. Only at six
o'clock, when the dancing began and Agnes was still
missing, it turned out that she had not spent the day
with either her sisters or any of her friends among the
merchant families. That was when the search began.

At first there was a certain amount of knowing laughter. Where was the mystery? What would you expect to
happen to a pretty lass who vanished on a public holiday? But Agnes was so quiet and modest, not given to
unseemly romping. Too proud of her beauty, people
said, or else too much afraid of her father. Besides
which, there were no young men absent from the
town that night, apart from one of Trabb's journeymen who had been given leave to go and visit his sick
mother.

'My poor lamb,' wailed Mrs Trabb. 'Likely she's been
carried off by the Egyptians.'

'Stop that foolishness, Martha!' snapped her husband.
'The silly maid's gone wandering in the woods and

sprained her ankle, I don't doubt. She's forever dreaming.'

He was more concerned than he cared to admit, and when the short night was over and the hunt started again, a small party of horsemen assembled, prepared to ride over the moor in pursuit of gipsies, vagrants or other bad characters liable to prey on lone women in solitary places. Giles and Bateman joined this party.

As they trotted uphill, following the track which led towards Charltonbury, Giles looked down into one of the pockets of lush green fed by the meandering river, and saw a line of men and boys pushing their way diligently through a tangle of trees and bushes. It must be hot work down there; he was glad he was not with them.

Then the rhythm of their slow progress changed. Someone stopped and pointed. They all began to converge. Shouts floated faintly upwards.

'They've found something,' said Giles.

The innkeeper from the Saracen's Head shaded his eyes.

'Praise God, I think they have.'

Down in the dank green wilderness of thicket and briar, Roger Trabb gazed at his sister. He had not been the first to see her. Several voices had sung out at once when something light and moving flickered through the maze of green. But he was the closest to her—mercifully, he thought as his mind groped with the horror of what must have happened to Agnes.

She was almost naked, stripped down to her shift, and that had been torn from waist to hem, so that one thigh was completely exposed, pearly skin mottled with dark bruises and dried blood. Her face was bruised too, and swollen; her eyes did not seem to focus.

'Agnes,' cried Roger, running to her.

She staggered forward and collapsed into his arms.

'He forced me,' she sobbed. 'Against my will. Tell my father he forced me.'

'Yes, yes,' said Roger, struggling out of his jerkin so that he could wrap it round her for decency's sake, and also because she was shivering and deathly cold. The rest of the party had now come up, including the youngest Trabb, Dickon, a boy of seventeen.

He at once wanted to know who had assaulted her. Agnes hid her face and would not answer.

'Don't trouble the poor maid now,' one of the older men advised him.

But Dickon was young and impulsive: he wanted the truth at once. 'Dear sister, tell me who the villain was that used you so.'

'Sir Giles Omberley,' whispered Agnes, and fainted.

The rescuers looked at each other, astonished and doubtful.

'I don't believe it,' said one.

'Why not? He's a known lecher. He'd spoil a maidenhead as soon as crack an egg, for all he's a gentleman born.'

'Damn his gentility! Why couldn't he leave my sister alone?'

'You'd better ask him, for here he comes, as bold as brass.'

The horsemen had come down from the high ground to see what was happening, Giles at their head. He took in Agnes's condition at a glance. He had seen plenty of victims of rape; it was one of the unpleasant aspects of soldiering.

He was about to commiserate with Roger, standing there with his sister in his arms, when he was taken aback by the sudden interest in himself. There were a great many people surging about his horse, and the younger brother had a very wild glint in his eye.

'Aren't you afeared to come near us, you damned villain? Or did you think you'd killed her? Shut her mouth?'

'What the devil do you mean?'

'You're the swine that ravished my sister.'

'You mind your manners, puppy!' said Bateman, moving closer to his master. 'That's a monstrous lie!'

'Who says I attacked your sister?'

'She told us so herself.'

'Then she must be . . . mistaken,' concluded Giles lamely.

He had been going to say 'out of her wits', but judged this would sound heartless to the hostile group surrounding him. Though out of her wits was exactly what the girl might be after what she had gone through. But why on earth should she have named him?

Thinking quickly, he said, 'You may not wish to believe me, but I can prove my innocence. How could I have committed this—this crime? I was at the banquet yesterday, and I dare say some of you saw me leave with Mr Rydal. I went with him to Waldon Harbour and stayed in his company till past ten o'clock. By that time Mrs Agnes had been missing many hours. However she spent them, it was not with me.'

This made a definite impression.

'You hear what his honour says.' The innkeeper spoke in the firm voice he used for calming down over-heated customers. 'Your sister was wandering in her mind, Dickon. And we should take her home instead of wasting time here.'

He dismounted, suggesting that Roger would find it more convenient to carry his sister on horseback, and the rest of the party prepared to escort them. They no longer threatened Giles: instead, they rather pointedly ignored him—apart from Dickon, who had to be almost forcibly removed, scowling furiously and still hoping for a quarrel.

Giles was left alone with Bateman.

'What a devil of a coil. Why should she tell such a story? She knows I never touched her!'

'Happen she wishes you had. She wouldn't be the first.'

'I don't want to hear any soldiers' bawdy,' said Giles repressively, though he knew enough about women to recognise that this might be true. They took lovesick fancies and sometimes clung to them when reality was too hard to endure.

'I'm going to the Priory,' he announced.

Bateman protested. 'I reckon you'd best keep out of Chelford for the present, sir. Ride back to Wansdown and stay there.'

'What—bolt for cover as though I'd done something to be ashamed of? Damned if I will! I've got one urgent matter to attend to first. Don't look so dismal, man. I shan't go right into the town, only to the Priory. What you can do for me is to make straight for Waldon Harbour and tell Mr Rydal what's happened, in case anyone comes asking questions.'

Bateman was doubtful, but he knew better than to argue.

Riding fast and cutting corners, Giles reached the Priory ahead of the slow cortège that was bringing Agnes back to her father's tall house nearby. Bridget had already spent some time over there trying to comfort Mrs Trabb. She had returned home merely to fetch a special elixir which might reduce the poor woman's palpitations, and was on the point of setting out again when Giles walked into the hall. One look at his face told the kind of news he brought.

'They've found her? Not—dead?'

'No, thank God. She's in a bad way, but I hope she'll recover. She was ravished, with a good deal of violence, and then left to lie out all night.'

'Oh, poor little Agnes. How terrible! Could she speak? Was she able to name the man?'

'She named me,' said Giles, gazing into Bridget's brilliant hazel eyes.

She gazed back at him, unwavering, for several seconds. Then she said, 'That's the purest folly. I'll never believe it.'

Giles had a feeling of physical relief stronger than any he had felt in all the tight corners of his life.

He said, 'I'm glad to hear it, Lady Rydal. I was afraid you might consider the whole sordid business only too likely.'

'For pity's sake, why should I?'

He did not answer in words. He simply glanced at the carved oak staircase on which Bridget had held Martin at bay while he was upstairs in bed with Martin's wife.

'Oh, that,' she said dismissively. 'But this is a different situation entirely. There's no comparison. Come, you must tell me more.'

She took him into the withdrawing-room and listened to his brief account of the scene in the woods.

'Your faithful henchman was right,' she said finally. 'You ought to have gone straight home. Chelford is no place for you until this matter has been cleared up. I don't perfectly understand . . .'

'You don't perfectly understand why the girl ever thought of naming me. Neither do I. I swear to you I've never made the smallest attempt to ensnare her. I don't care to dally with young virgins—I never have.'

Bridget could easily believe that. What she could not understand was why Giles had come to protest his innocence at the Priory, instead of going safely home. Perhaps he wanted her to reassure Lucy?

'I'll go and spy out the land at the Trabbs',' she said, 'and find out whether that unfortunate girl has come to her senses yet. You must stay here, Sir Giles. I'll tell them to bring you some refreshment.'

She was taking the short cut through Bennet's Alley when it struck her that Lucy would need no reassurance. Since Giles had spent the later part of yesterday at Waldon Harbour, she would know immediately that he could not have attacked Agnes Trabb. In which case, what curious impulse had brought him to the Priory?

While his sister was being gently taken home by their elder brother, Dickon Trabb and his cronies held a discontented conference at the roadside.

'I don't care what that arrogant bastard says,' he declared hotly. 'Agnes accused him. You heard her. And what cause had she to lie? He's just the sort of man who might have beguiled her with false promises and persuaded her to meet him privately.'

Some of the apprentices and young journeymen in the group had been snubbed by Agnes, and were ready to resent Omberley with his title and the glamour that surrounded a gentleman and a soldier. The saddler's son, more cautious than the rest, reminded them that Sir Giles was supposed to have gone to Waldon Harbour straight from the feast.

'I reckon he told us that to throw us off the scent,' said Dickon. 'He hoped we'd take his word for it because we shouldn't dare question a great man like Mr Rydal.'

They trailed back into the town, arguing about what to do next. Dickon was all for going to Waldon to test the truth of Sir Giles Omberley's statement. Several of his friends complained that they'd walked far enough already that morning, and they all knew that they ought to go back to work, now that the search for Agnes was over.

The fainthearts might have won, if they had not encountered a groom in the Rydal livery waiting in the Market Place.

Asked if his master was in town, the man nodded towards the shoemaker's shop. 'He's in there, talking to the Mayor.'

So they could ask their questions without a weary trudge to Waldon Harbour and back. They clustered together, stiffening each other's resolution.

Hearing that Agness was missing, Martin had come into Chelford to show neighbourly concern and had called first at the Mayor's house before going to see the Trabbs. Now he wished he hadn't, for Mr Honeycombe had no real information, and would go prosing on about the hypothetical fates that might have overtaken a young lass who was unwise enough to stray too far from home.

Martin was very tired and his head was aching. He had sat up drinking alone last night, after Giles had left him, trying to dull his senses. He had stumbled into bed, half stupefied, to be woken some time later by the sound of Lucy crying quietly in the dark. After that he lay awake, tormented by his own failures as a husband. He had failed to hold his wife's love, to avenge her infidelity —he hadn't even the courage to let those traitors know that he had discovered their secret. He had come to feel that he, too, was in the wrong, guilty by association. It was altogether intolerable.

He was vainly trying to interrupt the Mayor's endless monologue when an excited serving-maid popped her head round the door.

'They've found Mrs Agnes, ravished and left for dead, poor young creature. And Dickon Trabb's here, sir, asking to speak to Mr Rydal.'

'Merciful heavens,' exclaimed Honeycombe. 'What a terrible event! Show the boy in, Prudence. No doubt he brings a message from his father.'

On this assumption, Dickon was ushered into Martin's presence more easily than he had expected. He stalked in, hot and dirty from hours of searching, with three of his friends behind him, and began speaking without ceremony.

'Is it true, sir, that you can clear Sir Giles Omberley of the charge of assaulting my sister? She says it was Sir Giles that violated her, and he maintains that he was all day in your company. Is it true?'

Martin was mentally thrown off balance. Until a few weeks ago he would have thought such an accusation was incredible. Now that he was haunted by the image of Giles as a predator, a corrupter of virtue, nothing seemed too bad for him. He might just as well have added poor little Agnes to his victims.

Martin did not take in what he was really being asked: whether there was a discrepancy of times and places that would make Giles's guilt impossible. If the girl had accused him, it was unreasonable to suppose that she was lying, and Martin felt an additional sharpness of anger at his false friend's daring to appeal for protection to him, of all people.

'I am not Sir Giles Omberley's keeper,' he said coldly. 'I am indeed sorry for what has happened to your sister, but if she has brought a charge against him, it is no duty of mine to defend him.'

His face was pale and his voice colourless. The Mayor shot him a curious glance. Even if Mr Rydal could not prove Sir Giles's innocence, it seemed strange that he should make no attempt to challenge such a dreadful story. As though he knew his friend must be guilty—a terrible consequence of all this gallivanting about the Court and fighting in foreign parts. Good Sir William would have been very much afflicted by his godson's fall from grace.

Dickon and his friends saw nothing odd or ambiguous in Mr Rydal's reply, which merely seemed to confirm what they already suspected. They hurried back to their friends in the Market Place.

'He's guilty, just as I told you.'

'What are we going to do?'

'Hunt him out and make him sorry he laid hands on my sister.'

'Peter says he's skulking at the Priory. Shall we seek him there?'

'No sense in that. Her ladyship's servants will never let us get near him. I tell you what, though. He'll have to go home sooner or later. There's a place on the road to Wansdown where we can lie in wait for him. Then we'll have him at our mercy, undisturbed.'

Dickon had his own plans for meting out justice and knew very well that these would not be approved by the older generation: a pack of old women they were, frightened of breaking the law or offending the gentry. So he led his followers quietly out into the country without returning to his father's house.

When Bridget arrived there, she had found Agnes lying on a settle, wrapped in a blanket. She had been tenderly washed by her sisters, her cuts dressed and her bruises anointed. Her mother was gently combing broken twigs out of her beautiful fair hair. One of her sisters-in-law, standing just inside the door, told Bridget importantly that the apothecary had been but Agnes would not let him touch her.

'She's mortally afraid of every man who comes near her, my lady, and who shall wonder?'

Her brother stood by, helpless and awkward, while Thomas Trabb shuffled up and down the room, inveighing against the villainy of Sir Giles Omberley.

This was what Bridget had come to stop, though she was not quite sure how to begin.

'I hope you will soon be quite well again, Agnes,' she said, feeling a complete hypocrite, for how soon could any woman recover from such injuries to her body and spirit?

'I thank you, my lady,' whispered Agnes.

She was now in full possession of her senses, Bridget decided. When they found her wandering, terrified and half naked after a night in the open, she might have been nearly adrift on the borders of madness, but she had returned to sanity.

'Who was it did this terrible thing to you?'

The girl shut her eyes and said in a low voice, 'Sir Giles Omberley.'

'Your ladyship may well be astonished,' said the clothier. 'Indeed I count it a mercy that your revered husband is no longer here to witness the downfall of his favourite. That a gentleman born should commit so barbarous a crime . . .'

'I think there has been some misunderstanding. Leaving aside Sir Giles's honourable character, he had no opportunity yesterday to meet Agnes anywhere near Thorny Hollow, for directly after the feast he rode off with my nephew in the opposite direction and spent the rest of the day at Waldon Harbour.'

Bridget spoke with complete self-confidence, blissfully unaware of what Martin had been saying in the Mayor's house only a short time before. The Trabbs were shaken and uncertain. Everyone looked at Agnes, who plucked at the fringe of the blanket and looked away.

'Come, you will have to tell us the truth,' prompted Bridget.

'It is the truth.' The girl began to cry. 'It is! It is!'

'If any child of mine is found to be a liar . . .' began Trabb ominously.

Bridget felt intensely sorry for Agnes, but she must be persuaded to recant. Otherwise Giles would be saddled with this poisonous slander for the rest of his life. Hardening her heart, she tried again.

'Sir Giles has done nothing to injure you. Surely you cannot want him to hang for another man's crime?'

'To hang?' faltered Agnes. 'Oh no, I never wished —I thought no one would dare to touch a gentleman like him.'

Bridget thought what a fool the girl must be, but she kept her mouth shut.

'If it wasn't Omberley, who was it?' demanded the clothier.

Silence, broken only by Agnes's sobs.

'I suppose it was Jack Summers,' ventured one of her sisters at last.

'Summers!' roared Trabb. 'That idle jackanapes! Where is he? Send for him at once.'

'He's not here, Father,' said Roger. 'He's gone to see his mother at Charltonbury. You gave him leave.'

Trabb turned on his daughter. 'So you've been fornicating on the sly with a low-born rascal who's hardly out of his indentures. And telling lies in order to escape punishment. Well, you've been found out, and now you'll pay for your wickedness. You'll leave this house today, and you can beg your bread in the streets or starve for all I care. I'll have no more of you.'

The wretched Agnes lay shuddering under her

father's anger. Several of her family spoke up for her,
Roger pointing out that since his sister had been raped,
she could hardly be considered guilty of fornication.

This only made the tyrant angrier, and he said that if
any of his other children gave succour to her, he would
disown them, too. Mrs Trabb set up a wordless moaning,
too cowed to defy him.

'If Agnes may not stay here,' announced Bridget, 'I
shall take her with me to the Priory.'

She felt partly responsible for this horrible scene, even
though the silly girl had brought it on herself.

Trabb did not care for Bridget's suggestion. If Agnes
was taken in and cared for by the great lady of Chelford,
he himself would be made to look either a monster or a
fool. Blustering, he refused his permission.

'Since you have cast off your daughter,' Bridget told
him with biting scorn, 'you no longer have any authority
over her, and your permission is not required.'

This made the stern father change his tune and modify
his threats a good deal, but Bridget could see that Agnes
was petrified with fear of him. Clearly, it would be a
kindness to get her away from here. After some more
discussion, her plan was accepted, a servant sent running
with a message to Mrs Laver at the Priory, and soon
afterwards Bridget walked home, a little ahead of the
invalid.

She was hardly inside the house when she was seized
on by Elizabeth Laver.

'About Sir Giles, madam . . .'

'Where is he? I have some good news for him.'

'He left a short while ago. As soon as he heard you
were bringing Agnes here. He thought he had better not
be in the same house with her.'

That was understandable. He could not have guessed
that Agnes would confess the truth so quickly. But what

was Elizabeth saying now?

'. . . That boy Ned, the saddler's son, came here looking for him. He wanted to warn Sir Giles not to ride home alone. Dickon Trabb and some other wildheads are lying in wait for him on the Wansdown road and mean to do him a mischief. Unluckily the warning came too late.'

'Heavens!' exclaimed Bridget, horrified. 'I must go after him and stop him before it's too late. Elizabeth, you'll have to take charge of Agnes and put her to bed.'

'Certainly, madam. But surely you need not go yourself? Will you not send one of the men?'

Bridget was out of the house and running towards the stables before Elizabeth had finished speaking. She had no time to answer, and indeed could not have said clearly why it was imperative that she herself must make sure that Giles was safe. She ordered her groom to saddle a horse for her and be quick about it. She had not dressed for riding that morning, but was thankful that the moderately quilted kirtle that she wore about the house would not make it too difficult for her to sit on a side-saddle. It would have been much harder to manage the outrageously wide French farthingale hoop which she wore on formal occasions. She set off at a canter, wondering how far ahead of her Giles was, and where exactly Dickon Trabb and his crew had set their ambuscade.

Giles had some ten minutes' start of her, but he was in no hurry to get home. He had plenty to think about. He was glad he had called on Bridget Rydal, and gladder still that she believed him innocent of that vile charge of rape. He had not cared for Bridget at one time, seeing her as the mercenary young woman who had turned down a handsome fellow like Martin to marry a sick old man for his money and his title. Now he found her

enigmatic. The different sides of her nature did not fit.
And after she had saved him and Lucy from the consequences of his disgraceful folly, he had acquired a
growing respect and admiration for her, quite unlike the
ideas he generally held about women. He had taken
to calling at the Priory, anxious to overcome her
bad opinion and to prove that he was not altogether
contemptible.

She had not objected to his coming. She had even told
him, laughing, that he served a useful purpose. His
worldly wisdom and sharp wit frightened away her
suitors, who were all such blockheads.

He had never had an intellectual friendship with a
woman before, never thought it possible, yet it exactly
suited him now. He still missed Lucy and the pleasure of
making love to her, and though he was honest enough to
admit that this feeling would pass soon enough, there
were other feelings, a real remorse for the pain he had
caused her, and while he was conscious of her only a few
miles away and still so unhappy, it would be unforgiv-
able to hope for amorous encounters with anyone else.
His encounters with Bridget were entirely different, and
therefore permissible.

He was riding along on a slack rein, the way home so
familiar that he hardly noticed where he was. He passed
the right-hand fork to Waldon and went on down a lane
which twisted between high banks. Rounding a corner,
he saw a curious obstacle about ten yards ahead. The
lane was blocked by a handcart lodged sideways-on
between the two banks. He slowed to a walk, wondering
what the thing could be doing in such a place.

A slight movement made him look up. He caught sight
of Dickon Trabb high on the bank above him. One
glimpse was enough. He couldn't get past the cart. He
tried to swing round and go back the way he had come.

Then a rattle of stones came at him and his horse from both sides of the lane. The horse panicked and reared. Giles put up a hand to shield his eyes, and the lads came whooping down the banks, the tallest of them gripping him round the waist and dragging him to the ground.

Bridget, still some way behind, heard their shouts and came galloping on. She met the riderless horse, and as she turned the corner, saw a sight that chilled her blood.

Giles was down on his back with six young louts kicking him.

'Stop that, you villains!' she shouted. 'Let him go!'

She was too far off to do more than shout, but her arrival caused a diversion. The thunder of hoofbeats and a woman's voice startled the attackers into looking round. This gave Giles just enough time to roll out of their grasp and scramble to his feet. He was stronger and heavier than any of them, and a second later he was standing upright, his back against the solid bank, and defending himself with his fists.

Two of the youths took fright when they saw Lady Rydal, and tried to run away. Their cowardice was rewarded, for they got behind her horse, a notorious kicker, who kicked them both. One fell down, screaming that his leg was broken.

Giles had just floored another of his persecutors. Three remained, and they were pressing him hard. By now Bridget had come within reach.

Concentrating on Dickon, the ringleader, she struck him on the side of the head with her whip.

'Stop that, you murderers!' she was shouting. 'You've got the wrong man. Agnes has confessed—it was Jack Summers who ravished her. She's confessed, I tell you!'

The two young men who were not related to Agnes immediately gave up the fight.

Dickon said, 'I don't believe you,' and she hit him again. This time, she drew blood.

'That will teach you not to contradict a lady.'

Giles was gasping for breath, but still game. Deserted by his allies, Dickon was forced to listen while Bridget told him what had happened to Agnes, and what was likely to happen to him and his friends in the near future if Sir Giles chose to prosecute them for common assault.

There was a stunned silence when she had finished, and every eye turned imploringly on Giles. He was brushing himself down and feeling his bruises.

'I'll not lay a charge,' he said. 'If I had a sister who was treated so, I'd want to kill her ravisher. But you should not have taken the law into your own hands. Can you not see how justice may miscarry without a proper trial of evidence?' ('Good God, I sound like a schoolmaster,' he thought.)

'I'm sorry, sir,' muttered the now humble Dickon. 'I ask your pardon.'

'And so you should,' commented Bridget. 'Skulking here like footpads and kicking him when he was down.'

She sounded much less forgiving than the victim. Dickon eyed her warily. He turned once more to Giles.

'I reckon we acted too hasty. But when we asked Mr Rydal, and he said he couldn't speak for you . . .'

'I don't take your meaning. He did not deny that I was at Waldon Harbour yesterday?'

Dickon seemed confused and one of his friends broke in.

'Not in so many words, sir. He said he was not your keeper and that he had no call to defend you.'

There was an uncomfortable pause while they digested this.

Then Bridget said quickly, 'You cannot have made your question plain. No doubt Mr Rydal considered it great impudence your asking him about Sir Giles. He did not choose to discuss the matter.'

Young and inexperienced, frightened by their recent assault on the wrong man, they were ready to accept anything she told them. To more worldly ears Martin's answer sounded extraordinary, as though he was convinced of his own friend's guilt and would do nothing to protect him.

Concealing her dismay, Bridget commanded the prentices to take themselves off and be thankful they were not bound for the county gaol.

They straggled away towards Chelford dragging their handcart, a dejected little band. Giles's horse had recovered from its fright and ambled into view. He limped across to fondle the poor beast.

'How badly are you hurt?' asked Bridget.

'I've a bruise or two, nothing that hot water and liniment won't mend. Thanks to you, Lady Rydal. This is the second time you've rescued me from great peril.'

They surveyed each other. Both were dishevelled and dusty. Neither cared a straw for that. He thought how handsome she looked: a bright-eyed, courageous amazon. She had been surprised by the violence of her own feelings when she saw him on the ground.

'You might have been killed.'

He laughed, though he did not actually deny the fact. 'A fine end that would have been, after scaling the walls of Cadiz without a scratch, to be trampled to death in a country lane, and all for the sake of a girl I never even kissed.' Then he grew sober. 'I am sorry for her, but why in heaven's name should she drag me into her troubles?'

'Because she is a fool,' said Bridget crisply. 'There is an even stranger question. What can have possessed Martin? Why didn't he leap to your support as any true friend would have done?'

Giles hesitated. 'I am afraid he may have acted out of revenge.'

'Do you think he knows?'

'I'm convinced of it. That's why I stayed so long at Waldon yesterday: to give him the chance of accusing me if he wished to. When he said nothing, I thought he was keeping quiet in order to avoid a scandal and spare Lucy. Great heavens—Lucy! If he is prepared to turn on me, what will he do to her? I must go to Waldon directly, to make sure that she is safe.'

'On no account—that would be fatal!' said Bridget. 'You are the very last person who can shield Lucy from her own husband. I shall go to the great house and see them both.'

Lucy was at the virginals, trying to play a piece that Christopher Downey had written for her—'Mrs Lucy Rydal's Galliard'. It should have sounded lilting and serene, but she kept losing her place and hitting the wrong notes so that she produced the impression of some sick, stumbling creature who had forgotten how to dance. And that was how she felt, battling with her unhappiness. She blinked away her tears and stared at the sheet of handwritten music. She must go on practising. It was only by occupying her mind every waking hour that she could act like a rational creature. So when she was not supervising the servants, attending to the children, working in the garden or the stillroom or visiting the tenants, she tried to fill her time with music and reading.

Until lately she had done a great deal of beautiful embroidery, which had left her thoughts free to run over all the aspects of her happy life. Now she did not want to sew because she could not bear to think. She was not simply resisting a temptation to relive all those rapturous hours in the tithe-barn. She had resolutely put such dangerous memories behind her and honestly tried to recover her old contented innocent life at Waldon Harbour. Only everything felt different now, and the greatest difference seemed to be in Martin. She could take no pleasure in his company; a sort of dullness descended on them when they were together. Yet it was unreasonable to imagine that Martin had changed: she was forced to believe that the alteration was in herself. This was retribution. Her adventure with Giles had wrecked her peace of mind and ruined her marriage.

This morning at least she did have some kind of mental distraction in wondering about the disappearance of Agnes Trabb, and was dwelling on this, still seated at the virginals, when Martin walked into the great chamber.

She looked up as he came in, her fingers running over the keyboard, and a few more notes trickled out before she spoke. 'Is there any news? Have they found her?'

'Yes, they've found her. More dead than alive, by the sound of it. She was another of Giles's conquests, though less amenable than some. He took her by force and then abandoned her in Thorny Hollow.'

Lucy felt the blood literally draining away from her heart. 'You cannot mean *our* Giles?'

'Was he ever yours or mine?' asked Martin bitterly. 'If you ever thought so, you are in for a rude awakening.'

She was too horrified to take in the secondary implications, certain only that Giles would never resort to violence in his lovemaking or take a woman against her will.

She said so, aloud. 'And besides, how could he have been with Agnes yesterday? He was here with us.'

Martin had been dimly aware all along that there was something contradictory about the evidence against

Giles, but his furious jealousy left no room for logic.
There was no doubt that Agnes had been brutally and
shamefully ill used, and that she had named her attack-
er. He hated and despised Giles more than ever, and in a
curious way he found himself despising Lucy, who had
let herself be seduced by such a villain and was now
trying to defend him.

'You can leave off whitewashing that scoundrel's
character,' he said. 'I dare say he never raped you. He
did not need to.'

This time the gibe went home. She looked at Martin
and saw a stranger. Hostile, contemptuous, almost ugly,
if such perfect features could ever be ugly. The dark
eyes regarded her with an emotion she hardly dared to
recognise.

'How long have you known?' she whispered.

'Long enough to take your measure, you false-hearted
wanton.'

'Martin, I'm sorry! I never meant it to happen. And
it's over now, I promise.'

She was shaken and trembling, chiefly from remorse,
though she was afraid, too. She wondered what he
meant to do. She was in his power, and there was no one
she could turn to—certainly not Giles.

Martin seemed to read her thoughts, for he said,
'You'll get no help from your lover. He'll be hard put to
it to save his own skin. And he hasn't proved very
constant, has he? Even though you did say you'd feel the
same for ever. Did he ever say he loved you?'

Lucy did not answer. She had always known that Giles
did not feel for her with the intensity that she had felt for
him. All the same, she could not accept him as the villain
Martin was making him out to be, savagely violating that
fragile pretty girl. Guilty and desolate, she still had some
spirit left.

'I don't expect protection from anyone,' she said. 'How could I? This is between the two of us. I've broken my marriage vow, and I'm sorry. I am as much to blame as Giles, for I consented willingly. But if you think he raped that girl, you're wrong. He is incapable of such cruelty.'

'For God's sake, has he bewitched you?' Martin almost shouted. He took a step forward, raising his hand as though he meant to strike her. 'If you mention his name again, I shall—I shall . . .'

'What will you do, my dear Martin?' enquired the cool voice of his aunt by marriage.

They had neither of them heard her come in, and they were too deep in their own troubles to realise how odd she looked, powdered as though she had come through a cloud of dust, her bright hair escaping from an indoor linen cap, her skirt all bunched and creased.

'Lucy and I are privately engaged,' said Martin, not even trying to be civil. 'And I don't care to be interrupted. You have done enough wicked mischief already, allowing her to meet her paramour in your house.'

'Martin, what are you saying? Don't listen to him, Bridget.'

Lucy was now engulfed in a new humiliation. She had never dared to confide in Bridget, whom she admired so much but could not emulate. Proud as she was virtuous, Bridget would never have landed herself in such a plight and was bound to condemn those who did.

But Bridget, surprisingly, laid a hand on her arm, and said in a calming tone, 'There is no need to hide anything from me. As it chances, I discovered some time ago what was going on, but I have no taste for preaching homilies.'

Lucy gave a little gasp. Bridget squeezed her arm, and turned to Martin.

'I hope you will acquit me of taking part in some sort

of conspiracy. I fear you have fallen a prey to some very strange delusions. Why did you encourage Dickon Trabb to believe that Giles had ravished his sister?'

'I didn't encourage him. He knew it already. And why should I be expected to take Giles's part, after what he has done to me?'

'Because he is innocent.' Her eyes and voice were diamond hard; she confronted Martin like an avenging angel. 'Agnes has now admitted the truth. It was young Summers who assaulted her. There's no doubt she was afraid to let her father know she had been meeting one of his journeymen, so she pretended the man was Giles. She is such a simpleton that she supposed a gentleman of his standing would be above the law.'

Lucy gave a sigh of relief, but had the wit to keep her mouth shut. She was watching Martin.

'Well, I am glad that Giles has been cleared,' he said grudgingly.

Bridget was not going to let this pass.

'What a hypocrite you are! You wanted him to be sunk beyond redemption, didn't you? And you wanted him to pay for something he had not done. For you knew very well that he had no opportunity of meeting Agnes yesterday, yet you let those angry louts go off believing that he had lied to them, that he was so depraved that his closest friend would not speak a word on his behalf. So they set on him on the Wansdown road when he was riding home alone, dragged him off his horse and got him down on the ground, six against one.'

This time Lucy was not able to restrain a cry of anguish. 'How badly is he hurt?'

'A good many kicks and bruises. Nothing worse. By God's mercy, I—we were able to convince them of his innocence before matters had gone too far. Giles will soon be as right as rain. No thanks to Martin.'

He was gazing at her, speechless. He had flushed a dull, dark red.

'I never intended—I could not foresee such an outcome. And before you condemn me, think what I have endured. Does that not weigh in the balance? Your husband would not have dismissed adultery so lightly.'

'Neither do I dismiss it. What Giles did was very wrong. William would not have been proud of him. Nor of you either. There is a recognised way for a gentleman to redeem his honour. But,' said Bridget, made merciless by the terror she had felt when she saw Giles lying in the lane, 'perhaps you did not care to risk such an encounter? William always told me that Giles was the better swordsman.'

# CHAPTER
# FOURTEEN

'YOU NEED not fear for Lucy,' Bridget told Giles the following day.

Before leaving Waldon she had been able to send a reassuring message to him through Bateman (whom he had despatched there on a fruitless errand to Martin). Now she had arrived at Wansdown herself, to see what was happening at this male establishment which she viewed with some suspicion. Predictably, Giles's injuries seemed worse today than they had immediately after the affray. He had a black eye, was decidedly lame, and carried his right arm in a sling. He swore that the wrist was not broken, merely sprained.

He was limping up and down the solar in a distracted manner. Bridget sat in the window seat and watched him.

'Are you sure he won't beat the poor girl or lock her up in disgrace? He must be very angry.'

'He was being confoundedly self-righteous when I got there. By the time I'd done with him, he was in no state to cast stones at Lucy.'

'He has my sympathy,' said Giles with a faint grin. 'You have a very painful turn of phrase, my lady!'

'Why not say I am a shrew and have done for it?' Bridget hesitated. 'I fear I may have been too harsh, but he made me so angry, setting out to destroy your character behind your back while all the time pretending that he did not know you had been Lucy's lover.'

'I wish to God I'd never gone near her.'

Bridget said nothing. She thought of the scene at Waldon the day before, and of the talk she had had with Lucy after Martin had left them. Lucy, frozen in grief, saying stoically, 'I am being punished for what I have done, and I deserve no better. I would give anything to have prevented this hatred between Martin and Giles. Almost anything.' And then adding rather wildly, 'It cannot be so unnatural to love more than once.' Repeating this would do no good to either of them.

She reached out and ran a finger along the oak panel at the edge of the tapestry, frowning at the smudge of dust she collected.

'Your servants don't keep this place properly. You ought to have a woman here.'

'No honest woman would work for a man like me.'

'That's folly,' said Bridget briskly. 'I don't know why men of your stamp always try to make yourselves out worse than you are! Bragging about your dangerous reputations until someone takes you at your word, and then you are affronted. As you were yesterday.'

Giles stopped his pacing and fixed her with such an intense stare that she was afraid she had gone too far. Then he burst out laughing, and after a moment she laughed, too.

'More shrewd than shrew! That is your sharpest weapon: you will speak the truth.'

But he did not seem to mind, and listened meekly while she told him that he ought to employ a sober body, past the age for unseemly romping, to care for his linen and preserve his fruit, as well as keeping his menservants up to their work. She undertook to find him such a paragon. A sound outside in the lane caused her to look casually out of the window.

'Great heavens, there's Martin.'

'What's he doing?'

'He's tied his horse to the gatepost. I think he's coming in. No, he isn't. He's standing in the forecourt, looking up to the house.'

'I'd best go and talk to him.'

Bridget wondered uncomfortably whether her fatal gift for speaking the truth had driven the wretched Martin to come here belatedly and challenge Giles to a duel. Luckily Giles was in no state to fight at present. She watched him from above as he limped out of the house to confront his one-time friend, but she could not hear what they were saying.

They eyed one another warily like two animals. Then they both began to speak at once, interrupted each other, and fell silent again. At last Martin got out what he had come to say.

'I find I have misjudged you. I should not have given credit to such a slander. And I hope you will believe that I did not deliberately set on those young brutes to attack you.'

'No one in their senses would ever suppose that you did.'

'Bridget does. She told me that I was afraid to fight you myself because you are a better swordsman.'

'That's pure moonshine! Women never understand these matters.'

'Like enough she's right,' said Martin, staring at the ground.

Giles felt more conscience-stricken than ever. It was all wrong that Martin should have come here to offer him an apology. The boot should have been on the other foot.

'It is I who should have come to you for clemency,' he

said. 'But since you are here, will you not come in-doors?'

'I prefer to stay where I am.'

'He won't come inside my house,' thought Giles, and remembered with a shock that until a year ago it had been Martin's house, the first home to which he and Lucy had come within a week of their marriage, happy as two lovers in a pastoral, and no doubt believing that nothing would ever change or supersede that happiness. He felt increasingly guilty.

Looking over Martin's shoulder and unable to meet his eye, he said, 'If you want to fight, I shall be ready to meet you as soon as I have recovered the use of my arm. If that is what you wish.'

'No,' said Martin indifferently. 'All I need is an assurance that you will keep away from Lucy, and never attempt to see her privately or write to her.'

'I can promise you that. We had already decided, a month ago, that our . . . that this episode must be brought to an end. Indeed, I am truly sorry for the injury I have done you. It was all my fault. I hope you will be able to forgive Lucy, if you cannot forgive me.'

He paused, but Martin did not speak.

'She is so young still, and lived so little in the world . . .'

'I thank you, Sir Giles. I don't require to be told Lucy's life history. She has been my wife these five years, even if you both chose to forget the fact.'

Perhaps he had deserved that chilling reminder, thought Giles, but not surely the use of the title, the blighting formality. They stood dumb with misery, neither knowing what to do or say. Then Martin got on his horse and rode away.

He had no idea he had just won a victory by reducing Giles to the status of a worm.

He was too downcast himself to notice other people's feeling, his perceptions distorted by anger, grief and bewilderment. For he was totally bewildered. He could not understand the person he had become. A person he found hateful and contemptible.

After his first shattering discovery, he had decided to be patient and gentle with Lucy, to take no action which would cause her distress. To behave, in fact, with Christian forbearance. And somehow he had turned into a shouting, threatening bully, a mean resenter of slights, wanting to think the worst of Giles, actually hoping to see him disgraced. He was ashamed of his performance the day before, yet the injustice still rankled, for he recognised that if the whole story was known among men of their own kind, he would be condemned more severely than Giles, the adulterer.

A grey desolation now closed in on Waldon Harbour. Staring through windows continually blistered with rain, listening to the wind as it shrieked in the chimneys, Lucy felt isolated, always alone, always cold.

There were nearly eighty people living within the precincts of the great house and she knew them all, yet she felt quite remote from them as they moved around her in the hierarchic pattern of everyday life. Only her two little boys still seemed close to her, and she clung to them with more anxiety than comfort, for they had grasped, with the instinct of very young children, that something was wrong. Will had become naughty and Robin was often ailing. Lucy felt she was to blame.

Martin had not spoken another angry word to her since the scene in the great chamber. He hardly spoke to her at all and kept out of her way as much as possible.

They still slept in the same bed. They had to, if they wanted to avoid a scandal. This they managed with a certain cold-blooded ingenuity. Martin undressed in the adjoining closet and never entered the bedchamber until Lucy had blown out her candle and retreated inside the drawn curtains. Then he got into his side of the bed while she lay straight and stiff on hers, each being careful not to touch the other.

There they lay, together yet apart, as though imprisoned in separate coffins within the same tomb. And they both thought, 'This is how it will be from now on, for ever.'

The summer of 1596 was the worst in living memory. Storms tore across the country, flooding rivers, tearing up trees by the roots, ruining crops and spreading disaster. The English fleet under Essex and Raleigh, setting off once again to harass the Spaniards, was nearly sunk off the coast of Cornwall. To Giles it seemed that this appalling weather had one advantage. There were few of the usual hawking and hunting parties, or convivial meetings in country houses, so the fact that he never went near Waldon Harbour now escaped the notice of their neighbours.

He spent a good deal of time with Bridget. Their almost daily meetings had become a regular pleasure to them both. This did cause comment. As someone pointed out innocently to Lucy, it looked as though Sir Giles was about to capture a rich prize without risking his life on salt water.

Lucy did not believe that rumour. She had always thought that Giles and Bridget rather disliked each other, until one day in Chelford she caught sight of them coming out of the new almshouses together and laughing hilariously at some private jest. Lucy fled down a side street, pain like a physical sensation tightening round her heart.

If Giles had known, he would have been sorry to hurt her, though he could have said truthfully that the friendship between himself and Bridget was entirely platonic.

As the weeks went by, he began to wish it was not so. He found her extremely desirable and wondered why it had taken so long to see through her shell of uncaring independence. Behind it she was entirely feminine and beguiling, and he would have liked to make love to her, but dared not try. He was a little in awe of her tongue and her temper, an unusual sensation for him. Yet he could not keep away from her.

'How strange it is,' he thought one day in September, riding with her on the moor above Wansdown. 'I would sooner be up here in the teeth of a gale with this contrariwise young woman than sporting on a bed of roses with Helen of Troy.' Amused by the comparison, he laughed. She turned and asked him why.

'I was thinking how strangely we choose our pleasures,' he improvised. 'If I were obliged to ride out on such a day as a matter of duty, I should feel myself confoundedly ill used.'

She laughed too, and he thought how well she looked, erect in the saddle, the blood tingling in her cheeks as she faced into the wind.

It took him several more days to recognise the name commonly given to his curious state of mind. For the first time in his misspent career he had genuinely fallen in love.

Summer passed unlamented into autumn while he was still considering this extraordinary circumstance and wondering whether there was any hope for him. Some time in the future, perhaps, if he went very carefully and managed to live down his previous follies.

*       *       *

'I hope to have my newly-built coach sent down from London next week,' Bridget told Giles just before Michaelmas.

'Whatever made you order such a conveyance? A coach is very well in town, but down here you will be continually sticking in the mud or losing a wheel. It's not as though you disliked riding.'

'Very true,' she said equably. 'But only think how jealous Lady Arcot will be of my insufferable grandeur. And how the good Bolderstons will moralise over my fine lady ways. I must have a new toy. I have finished building my almshouses, and there is nothing more I can do here.'

They were strolling up and down the one remaining arcade of the Priory cloister in the October light that was warm and golden after the dreary summer. Giles glanced sideways at his companion. He thought she had more energy than she was able to spend. This house must seem small after Waldon Harbour, and most of the land Sir William had left her was leased out to tenants.

She had property of her own in the county of Northampton, and it surprised him that she never went there to see what her steward was about. Not that he wished her to go. It pleased him to have her permanently settled in Chelford, and he had begun to hope seriously that he might stand a chance with her.

'I'm short of space here,' she said, her mind still fixed on building. 'There's a disadvantage you don't suffer from. You ought to enlarge the manor house. Throw out a wing on either side. You'd have to remove the dovecot and level the ground, but that would be a small matter.'

Giles would have resented this from anyone else. He enjoyed listening to advice from Bridget, even when he did not mean to take it.

'And what would you have me do with my new wings?
I have all the rooms I need already.'

'You could make a better eating parlour and a wider
staircase. And a long gallery.'

'What should a bachelor do with a long gallery? They
are meant for family festivities, and for ladies and
children to exercise in bad weather.'

'I suppose you will not be a bachelor for ever, Sir
Giles.'

He took a deep breath. Was this the opportunity he
was waiting for, coming sooner than he had expected?

He said, 'I've never seen but one woman I should wish
to marry, and she wouldn't have me. Would she?'

They both stopped walking. Bridget had lost some of
her composure.

'I spoke at random. You must not read any special
meaning into my words.'

All the same, thought Giles, a woman who had refused so many suitors would not lay herself open to such
a question, and then show so much agitation, if she was
merely indifferent. Having gone so far, he decided to
press on.

'I think you must know that I love you,' he said. 'If you
don't, it can only be your own want of vanity that has
misled you. For the past three months and more, I have
cared only to please you, longed only to be with you.
You cannot have a high opinion of me, but at least you
know the worst there is to know. And if you could love
me in return, I could be a faithful husband to you,
Bridget . . .'

'Oh, do stop talking! I don't want to hear any more.'

He stood gazing at her, his dark brows drawn
together. She sounded deeply distressed, twisting her
hands together like an awkward girl. He did not know
what she was thinking, but a man of his experience could

not fail to guess what she was feeling. He thought he could convince her in a language more potent than words.

He took her in his arms and kissed her mouth. For a moment he believed he had won, as her lips parted under his and her body seemed to soften.

Then she wrenched herself out of his grasp, exclaiming, with a sharp return of the old Bridget, 'Who gave you leave to treat me as one of your lightskirts?'

'You did not dislike it,' he retorted, more frank than chivalrous. 'And you know very well I am not playing country games with you, sweetheart. I love you, and I want to marry you.'

'Well, you are not going to marry me, so there's an end of it.'

She had turned away from him, leaning against one of the pillars of the cloister. He was baffled by the discrepancy between her words and her emotions: a less accomplished lover would have taken No for an answer more easily. Giles was sure she was fighting her inclinations. He searched for a possible reason, and thought he had found one.

'Are you afraid to surrender your independence?' He addressed her rigid shoulders and the back of her head. 'You've been your own mistress for more than a year, and I can see it must go against the grain to accept the dominion of a new husband. I can promise you I should not dream of trying to manage your great possessions without consulting you on every point. I have too much respect for your judgment. You have only to trust me.'

'Why should I?' she burst out violently without turning round. 'Why should I trust you in any capacity?'

It took him a few seconds to make out the full meaning of what she was saying, and then the humiliation turned him to stone. Why should she trust him, after all? She had watched him betray others who had put their trust in him. What had he ever done to persuade her that he would make a faithful husband, or even that he would keep his word and give her a say in her own affairs once her money and property had passed into his hands? In a mood of bitter self-disgust he saw where he had made his mistake. He had won her liking and charmed her senses, so that he thought she had accepted him as a reformed character. But he was wrong. Even if she believed that his declaration of love was sincere, she expected him soon to change his mind, no more constant to her than he had been to Lucy. She thought he was a man of straw, and who could blame her?

'I'm sorry,' he said at last. 'I have been presumptuous and importunate. I shan't trouble you again, madam.'

Then he went away.

She heard his footsteps receding. When she was sure he had gone, she slipped back into the house, avoiding Elizabeth Laver and Agnes, who was still staying here under her protection. She ran upstairs, shut the door of her chamber behind her, and flung herself on the bed in a torrent of weeping.

# CHAPTER
# FIFTEEN

'I THOUGHT you would wish to know, sir,' said Christopher Downey, the secretary, appearing in Martin's study, 'that Lady Rydal's coach has been sighted coming up the combe.'

He spoke with mock solemnity, as though reporting the approach of a second Armada.

'Then I must be there to greet her,' said Martin. 'Does Mrs Rydal know?'

'Yes, sir. She has taken the children to observe her ladyship's progress.'

'They will enjoy the treat at all events,' Martin remarked, as they crossed the enclosed court.

He could not imagine why Bridget had ordered an expensive coach to be built for her and brought down from London, but since she was about to pay them a formal visit, he must do the honours. He had not seen a great deal of her since their stormy encounter at the end of June, though there had never been an open breach and he knew how to behave towards his uncle's widow.

When he reached the gatehouse he found a large company assembled, not merely Lucy and the little boys, but a good many of the servants and most of the inhabitants of Waldon village, all gazing down the green bed of the combe towards the two great white horses advancing at foot pace and dragging behind them a large, heavy object which swayed from one tipsy angle to the next over the rough track. It looked a little like the Ark of the Covenant, he thought irreverently.

He had seen and ridden in plenty of coaches in London, and so had Lucy, but such a thing was a novelty to many of the spectators who raised a cheer when at last it drew up in front of them.

The painted yellow wheels and black body were already rather dirty; the windows had leather flaps to keep out the dust. Martin opened the door, which was decorated with the family crest, and helped Bridget down.

'This is a very splendid conveyance,' he said. 'I hope you had a comfortable journey.'

'An eventful one. We have been barked at by every dog and shied at by every horse we met on the way. And Agnes is feeling seasick.'

Agnes was also being helped out, and looked decidedly wan.

Everyone wanted to inspect the coach, and Bridget was very ready to show off her new possession. Lucy suspected that she already knew it was going to prove impractical in the country, but was not prepared to say so. When the little boys clamoured for a ride, she maintained that she had come all the way to Waldon Harbour especially to give them this treat. She got back into the coach with Will and Robin, and they drove ceremoniously up and down in front of the gatehouse for several minutes.

Martin then escorted her indoors to dine. Lucy followed with Agnes.

She always found it difficult to get a word out of Agnes, and wondered how much longer she would be staying at the Priory. Thomas Trabb had long ago recovered from his rage against her. His remaining wrath was directed towards the journeyman Summers, who had not been seen or heard of since the day of the rape. The Trabbs would have been glad to have Agnes home, but she was still so nervous and showed such a dread of her father that Bridget was too kind-hearted to tell her she ought to go. She might once have gained a little polish from living under the patronage of a great lady, but this had come too late. Still in low spirits, she was growing heavy and blowsy, and her exquisite prettiness had gone.

'I used to think I should like to ride in a coach,' she said to Lucy. 'I did not know it would make me so queasy. I hope her ladyship is not offended.'

'You need not repine. It is no disgrace to feel sick in a coach: plenty of people do.'

When they were seated at the dinner-table, Martin said to Bridget, 'What do you think of Giles's intention to shut up his house and go abroad? Are you surprised?'

He had heard the news yesterday from one of the Bolderstons, and had been wondering ever since how to pass it on to Lucy. He was afraid of sounding either heartless or triumphant. He jumped at this chance of mentioning the matter to a third person in Lucy's presence, and he failed to notice that she was actually less disturbed than Bridget.

'Giles is going abroad?' Her knife squeaked on the pewter plate. She laid it down beside the meat she was cutting, and crumbled her bread with nervous fingers. 'Are you sure? What does he mean to do?'

'Enlist as a volunteer in the Netherlands, so he told Humphrey Bolderston.'

Martin was covertly watching his wife, and she was watching Bridget, noting the quick flush that had come and gone leaving her chalky pale. To Lucy herself the news had come as a muffled blow, anxiety made less real by months of separation. So he was not going to marry

Bridget after all. Lucy had schooled herself to accept the possibility—she could not bear to be jealous of Bridget. Now it seemed as though she had no cause.

There was an awkward little hiatus in the talk at the table. Dishes were assiduously handed, a savoury smell of venison filled the air. Lucy was searching for something to say when they were all startled by a sharp cry from Agnes, who slumped forward and nearly slipped from the bench. Her face was contorted and she was retching violently.

Walter Rathbone caught and held her; Lucy jumped up and went to his aid. It was absolutely necessary to get her away from the dinner-table. They took her into a small room behind the parlour and helped her into a chair. Rathbone was sent away and the women hovered round her.

'It's the fault of that damned coach,' said Bridget. 'My dear child, I did not understand how badly it affected you.'

Agnes moaned and clutched her stomach.

Lucy was untying her laces. A moment later she realised that the ride in the coach had been only the culmination of Agnes's troubles. She glanced at Bridget, who was looking puzzled. Bumping over bad roads might make anyone sick and dizzy, but her protégée was clearly in great pain.

She asked, 'What did you eat before we came out this morning?'

Lucy said in a low voice, 'She's with child. Did you not know?'

'No!' exclaimed Bridget. She took a step back. 'Indeed I did not. I asked her, and she assured me there was no sign. But it was always on the cards. That villainous brute—how long is it? Fourteen weeks? Is she going to miscarry?'

'I think so. It's not so simple, however.' Lucy leant
over the hunched figure in the chair. 'How far gone are
you, my dear?'

Speaking through clenched teeth, Agnes said something about St Peter's Day.

'That won't do. At the least you are carrying a four-
month child. Have you taken any steps to be rid of it?
You must tell me, for your own safety.'

She heard Bridget give an exclamation of horror and
disbelief.

'I swear I've taken nothing,' sobbed Agnes. 'I didn't
know who to ask, and it's all of five months. Oh Jesu, I
have been so wicked—my father will kill me!'

And that, of course, accounted for her continued
fears, her reluctance to go home. When Jack Summers
ravished her on the feast day she had not been the
innocent they all supposed. Some weeks earlier she had
been the secret and presumably willing partner of the
man who got her with child. And when her father knew
the truth, he might not actually kill her but he would
make her life unbearable.

Then he wouldn't find out, thought Lucy with a
sudden determination. She had a fellow-feeling for the
unhappy Agnes. They had both fallen from grace in the
same way, though Agnes was less culpable: she had not
deceived a loving husband.

'Take heart,' she told the weeping girl. 'We'll care for
you. Your father need never know.'

The birth of a living child would have raised complica-
tions, but a five-month baby could not survive. If they
managed the business discreetly, the story need not
come out.

She said to Bridget, 'Will you stay here while I go and
speak to Rachel?'

She left the room without waiting for an answer.

Rachel was her head laundrymaid, a capable nurse who sometimes deputised for the village midwife.

In the dark passage behind the dining parlour she almost collided with Martin.

'What ails her?' he asked. 'Is she gravely ill?'

'She's just about to miscarry.'

'As a result of the rape? Did Bridget not know?'

'She says not. And it wasn't the rape.'

Lucy saw she would have to explain. She could not put her plan into action in Martin's house without telling him what was happening. Suppose Agnes died? There would be awkward questions to answer.

So she repeated what she had discovered, which was not much, adding, 'I want to protect her from her father's wrath if I can. You know the fate he will think fit for her if he finds out: hell on earth and hell hereafter. She is terrified out of her wits, and she is going to lose her baby. Surely that is enough.'

She could not make out Martin's expression in the dim light, and it struck her that her wish to condone another young woman's immorality might draw some withering comment from him.

But Martin merely said, 'You can't leave her where she is. You'll have to move her. Is she fit to walk?'

'If we support her. I thought we might take her to one of the unused chambers at the far end of the west wing. Although I am afraid this will strike the servants as odd and they will all begin to talk.'

'Not if you put it about that Agnes has contracted some kind of rash, and you fear a contagious disease. That will kill two birds with one stone. It will explain why she is being nursed in a most isolated corner of the house, and it will discourage anyone from hanging round in idle curiosity and seeing or hearing enough to give the game away. They won't do that if they think she may be sickening for smallpox or the plague.'

'Martin, that is a surpassingly good scheme!'

Lucy's voice was warm with admiration, very different from the strained civility that was usual between them now. 'Agnes will be safe from all suspicion.'

'I hope so,' he said, and stood aside to let her pass.

Lucy decided which of the distant chambers was to be used, confided in Rachel and sent her there with old sheets to put on the bed. Next she took Margery into the stillroom and they measured out a restorative draught for a woman in labour and a herbal infusion to quench the flow of blood. She returned to the little room where she had left Agnes with Bridget, and as she approached the door, Bridget came out.

Lucy began to speak of the arrangements she had made, and of Martin's inspired plan to ensure secrecy. She was too preoccupied to notice that Bridget was restless and inattentive, and she finished by saying, 'We had better move Agnes to the west wing directly.'

'You need not count on me to take part in your play-acting,' declared Bridget in a high, unnatural voice. 'Did you suppose I should willingly offer myself as a midwife to that slut? Attend on her heavings and sweatings, listen to her wailing—oh, and I dare say you would like me to wash her soiled linen into the bargain! Well, you ask too much. I'll have no more to do with the little strumpet!'

And Bridget pushed past, her face rigid with some overwhelming passion, leaving Lucy gazing after her in dumb astonishment.

She had never seen Bridget behave like this or imagined she could fail in a crisis. The sound of Agnes crying behind the closed door brought her to her senses. This was no time to stand about wondering. There was too much to be done.

\*       \*       \*

The rest of Lucy's day passed wearily, shut up in the barely furnished chamber in which Agnes groaned and laboured on the uncurtained bed. She and Rachel ministered to her, Margery lit a fire to heat water, and the chimney smoked abominably. Agnes did not complain. She was braver than Lucy expected, but a miscarriage was always a melancholy event, and this one seemed sadder than ever, paradoxically because everyone saw it was a blessing not even in disguise.

The tiny dead baby was malformed. Lucy whisked it out of sight in case the mother should ask to see it. She did not do so. Her ordeal had weakened her and she was very low. They did their best to make her comfortable, and at last she went to sleep.

Margery and Rachel were to sit with her by turns. Lucy went back to her own chamber. She felt hot and dirty. She had washed carefully before leaving the west wing, yet the smell of smoke and blood and travail seemed to hang round her, in her clothes and her hair. She began to wonder what had become of Bridget, whose defection seemed more extraordinary than ever. How could she abandon the girl she had protected so generously for the last three months, and speak of her in such brutal terms? It was true that Agnes had behaved badly, deceiving her and lying about her pregnancy. 'But Giles and I behaved worse,' thought Lucy, 'and she rallied to our defence without a moment's hesitation.'

A thought stirred uncomfortably in the recesses of her mind. She had not asked Agnes who was the father of her child; the time had not been propitious, but she thought it very likely that Bridget had made some enquiries while she was closeted with Agnes in the little room behind the dining parlour. It was just then she had become so unaccountably angry, and if Agnes had identified her lover, surely there was only one person whose name would have such an effect on Bridget?

'I can't bear it,' thought Lucy, flinching away from the idea. 'Surely he would not have treated me so?' For if Giles had been the father of that child, he must have been Agnes's lover back in May when he and Lucy were meeting almost daily at the tithe-barn, when she, at least, believed their love would last.

'He wouldn't have played me false,' she said aloud, standing in her chamber and staring through the window into the dusk.

Yet she could not help remembering how Agnes had begun by accusing Giles of the savage assault made on her by Jack Summers. Was that because she was in love with Giles, her first seducer, and hoped that he would marry her? She was already pregnant—the wonder was that she hadn't lost her baby then.

Lucy was not a fool: she had never expected Giles to remain faithful to her after their separation. Indeed she saw no reason why he should. All the same, she had cherished the illusion that so long as they were lovers, their happiness had been precious to him. It was intolerable to think of him slipping off between their secret meetings to lie with that empty-headed little doll.

Her throat thickened with tears and she felt imprisoned within the tyranny of her own body, her memory acting as an instrument of torture. Even the walls of the great house seemed to close in on her. She must get out into the fresh air.

Beyond the bedchamber there was a spiral stair, and at its foot a doorway opening straight on to a grass terrace that overlooked the stream as it plunged and bubbled through the combe.

Lucy ran down the stone steps and let herself out into the freedom of an October evening. Dusk filtered the colours of walls and trees, so that their grey and green

deepened into violet, swelling the bulk of their shapes
and shadows. A steady rain was falling. She drew a deep
breath and let the seething sounds of water soothe her
hurt mind. She pulled off her cap and let the needle-
points of rain tingle on her scalp and wash away the
smoke from her hair. She did not notice the cold, but
spread her arms and closed her eyes, wanting only to be
cleansed. The rain was now coming down in torrents,
but she did not care. She felt refreshed and lightened
as though she were shedding the weight of her own
existence.

In this trance-like state she became aware of a hand on
her shoulder, and Martin's voice saying, 'Lucy, what are
you doing here? Come indoors, you're soaked to the
skin!'

She opened her eyes and blinked at him through
lashes that quivered with beads of rain.

'Do come along, for pity's sake!'

He shepherded her in with the exasperated affection
of a parent with a wilful child. She was entirely docile.
Once inside, she realised how wet she was, for rivers of
water were running off her clothes on to the flags.

'You must change your dress immediately,' said
Martin, still fretting about her. 'Or, better still, why do
you not go straight to bed? You look worn to death. I
gather all is well with Agnes: she's in no danger?'

Lucy discovered she was immensely tired. They had
started to climb the spiral stair when a thought struck
her. She stopped and looked down at Martin over her
shoulder.

'Is Bridget still here?'

'Yes. She will have to remain until Agnes is recovered
and we are able to say that the fear of infection was a
false alarm. It would look very odd otherwise. Though I
don't think she was best pleased when I made that plain

to her. Is it true that she gave you no assistance in the sickroom?'

'None.'

'I find that very inconsiderate. We did not invite that wretched girl to come and miscarry in our house.'

Lucy had begun to climb the stairs again. She walked into the bedchamber and said, without turning round, 'I think Bridget must have asked Agnes who it was fathered her child.'

'What does that signify?'

'I think it may have been Giles.'

'Giles?' repeated Martin with such astonishment that she did cast him a fleeting glance and then looked away again. 'But his innocence was proved. No, to be sure. This has nothing to do with the rape.'

There was a long pause. Lucy could almost hear him calculating the date of the child's conception and making the same deduction as she had done. She dreaded what was coming next. But he spoke quite moderately.

'I think you are jumping to conclusions. Unless you have any further evidence?'

'You did not hear how Bridget disclaimed any future intention of caring for Agnes after I had left them alone together. Agnes must have told her some part of the truth, and I cannot think of anything else that would have made Bridget so angry and so heartless. Giles has been paying court to Bridget lately, as I dare say you know, and I have just thought—Agnes has been there at the Priory all along, and if she was ever his mistress . . .' Lucy's voice trailed off miserably.

Martin said, 'It is all conjecture, nothing more. And you are shivering. I'll send your woman to you without more delay.'

He summoned Lucy's maid, with instructions that a warming-pan must be brought to heat the bed, and a posset of hot milk. Then he retired to his study without troubling to light the candle. It was from this window that he had seen Lucy in the October twilight abandoning herself to the relentless purifying rain as though she was the sacrificial victim in some pagan ritual. And all because she thought Giles had played her false at the zenith of their love.

He sat for a long time wrestling with his loneliness before he went to look for Bridget.

She was not in the great chamber, but he found her pacing up and down the long gallery.

He said abruptly, 'There is a question I should like to ask you.'

'Very well. What is it?' She sounded both defiant and apprehensive.

'Did Agnes tell you who fathered her child?'

'Why, it was Jack Summers to be sure. Who else should it be?'

The answer was so spontaneous and there was such a note of relief in her voice that he was sure she was speaking the truth. He wondered in passing what she had been expecting.

'There was never anyone but Summers,' she said. 'It's a sorry tale, and I learnt the whole of it only today. Agnes was left hanging about at home because her father could not get her a husband he considered worthy of her beauty and his own importance. She drifted into an intrigue with Summers. He persuaded her to run away with him. They were to leave on St Peter's Day. But Agnes had small taste for such an adventure. She decided that she did not love Summers, who was often rough and unkind to her. She was not yet certain of her condition, and hoped for the best, as such improvident girls always do. She went to the trysting-place, only to tell him she had changed her mind. Summers was so maddened with rage and disappointment that I suppose she was lucky to escape with her life.'

It was a sorry tale indeed, but it explained why Agnes had lied about the man who had ravished her: she did not want him caught because he could give her away. And perhaps it also explained why Summers never had been caught. Perhaps he had taken his own life in a fit of remorse, and his body might be lying undiscovered on some remote river bank or in some hidden crevice of the hill. Poor devil! thought Martin. There could be no justification for rape, yet he had a certain sympathy with the miserable Summers. He knew, better than most, what it was like to be rejected by a woman he loved who had once said she loved him.

He saw Bridget watching him, and felt suddenly angry with her. She had left Lucy to deal with all the sordid business of Agnes's lying in, not because she was in the grip of a deep personal anguish but simply because she had been misled by the girl's spurious innocence and made to look a fool.

'I hope you don't mean to abandon Agnes altogether?' he said bluntly. 'Or at least that you will not abandon her in this house.'

'I shall do no such thing,' retorted Bridget, indignation masking a touch of guilt. 'I wonder you need to ask.'

'It seemed to Lucy that the poor girl was so sunk in your displeasure that you were no longer willing to put yourself out on her behalf.'

'And let her make what she chooses of that,' thought Martin. He was pretty sure the shaft had gone home.

He went back to Lucy, to find that she had drunk the hot milk and fallen into a sleep of sheer exhaustion.

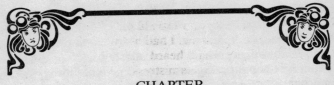

# CHAPTER
# SIXTEEN

WHEN LUCY woke next morning and parted the bed-curtains, she immediately saw Bridget sitting on a chest under the window. She calculated the slant of the light coming through the leaded panes, and jerked herself upright.

'I overslept. Why did no one wake me?'

'You were very tired. Martin gave orders that you were not to be disturbed.'

'Oh. Do you know how . . .'

'How Agnes is? Better for her night's rest. I have been to see her. She is somewhat doleful, but she will soon mend. There's no sense in blaming fools for their folly.'

There was a short silence, then Bridget said, 'You think I behaved with great cruelty yesterday. There is something I must tell you.'

'Has it to do with Giles?' asked Lucy, pulling up the quilt as though it would protect her from the onslaught of facts she might not want to hear.

'Giles? No. It has to do with me. Did you never wonder why I married William?'

Lucy did not reply. She would have found the answer embarrassing, even if she had not been taken so completely by surprise.

Bridget said, 'I know what was generally believed. That I thought the uncle a better bargain than the nephew because I hoped to cut Martin out by having a son of my own. Coming down here as a stranger, I was not supposed to know how little likelihood there was of that. But of course I knew. I had not been in the house two days before I had heard all the gossip about William's two wives and his mistress and his failure to get children. My maid Mercy collected all the servants' talk and passed it on. So I seized the opportunity of becoming Lady Rydal.'

Lucy was more mystified than ever. She could not see any logic in this explanation. Could Bridget be hinting at some freak of nature in herself, a reluctance to surrender her virginity? The idea seemed too ludicrous to consider. Bridget had never been prudish. In any case the fact that a man was childless did not make him impotent. Lucy was sure that the marriage had been consummated.

'I thought you were happy with Sir William,' she said at last, because she could not think of anything else.

'So I was. He was very good to me.' And then, taking the point, 'Oh, you are far astray. *That* has never been the trouble.'

'What, then?'

Bridget sat as still as an effigy on a tomb. Outlined against the light, it was impossible to read her expression.

She said in a low voice, 'The miserable fate of womankind. The duty of bearing children. I want no part in it. The whole process sickens me.'

'Great heavens, why?'

The words slipped out from sheer astonishment. Lucy had never heard anyone say such a thing before. And that it should be Bridget of all women, strong courageous Bridget with her proud descent and her sense of the obligations of a great lady.

'Why? Because I am a coward, my dear Lucy, that's

why. I dread to think of all that blood and filth.'

The words seemed to be torn out of her in a paroxysm of fury and shame. She turned away, and pretended to stare out of the window.

After a baffled pause, Lucy asked, 'Have you ever seen a child born?'

For perhaps she had never done so. And though that business with Agnes yesterday had been dismal enough, the arrival of a healthy, longed-for baby was very different. Lucy remembered that when her own two sons were born, Bridget had given some plausible excuse for not being on hand. Now it seemed as though she had kept away deliberately and so increased her fear of the unknown.

But Bridget's answer, when it came, was a shock.

She said stonily, 'I am not as ignorant as you may suppose. I was alone with my sister and helped to deliver her of a stillborn child when she was thirteen years old. I was seven.'

'Seven?' repeated Lucy, horrified. 'How could such a terrible thing happen?'

Bridget shifted a little and sat staring into the past. She began to talk fluently.

'After my mother died, my father spent most of his time at Court, leaving us with servants in the country. We had a governess, a stupid woman who thought of nothing but her health. You might say we were neglected. I was happy enough hanging round the stables or the mews. Mary fell a prey to one of the house musicians, an Italian who taught her lessons in love when he should have been teaching her to play the virginals. When she found herself with child, she had no one to confide in. She let matters drag on, hoping for some miracle, like silly Agnes. At last she plucked up courage and went to a white witch in the village, seeking a remedy. By then it was too late. She was six months gone.'

Bridget paused, remembering. 'There's an old tower at Farfield, part of the castle that fell into disuse when my grandfather built the new house. I used to play there, a game of King Arthur and his knights. One day as I drew near the place, I heard screams coming from within. Mary was lying on the ground, writhing in agony. The witch's brew had sent her into premature labour. I was very frightened. I thought she had been poisoned, and I think at first she thought so, too. We were both so ignorant. When she did try to tell me, she kept crying out in pain and I was too stupid to grasp what she meant. Of course I knew how babies were born, but it never struck me that Mary might have one. She was too young even to be married. When I understood at last . . .'

She broke off, her throat working convulsively as she fought to repel the ugly and distressing images.

'Say no more,' Lucy told her quickly. 'I can guess how it was. And yet your sister survived?'

'Yes. I fetched our old nurse, and helped her to stanch the blood and afterwards to wash the stone floor. Mary was carried indoors wrapped in a blanket, and it was given out that she'd fallen while walking among the ruins. My father never learnt the truth. Those of our servants who were in the know kept Mary's secret. They were afraid for their own skins; they should have taken better care of her. Mary recovered sooner than I did, which has always seemed strange to me. I used to have nightmares in which those scenes were happening over and over again, sometimes to her, sometimes to me. By the time I was ten, I'd sworn to myself that no man should ever put me in the danger of bearing a child.'

'I am not surprised,' said Lucy. She was full of anger

and pity for the little girl of seven years who had been dragged into such an episode.

She could not blame the older Bridget for the fear that had been festering all those years like an abscess in the mind because it could not be admitted openly. To say she did not want children would have been regarded as a blasphemy, a rejection of God's purpose in creating her and all other women. Had Mary Montresor made no effort to comfort her younger sister? Lucy asked the question.

Bridget shrugged. 'Mary was anxious only to forget. Well, so was I. She was able to manage it: I was not. Mind you, she'd been in great pain, and pain acts like a drug on the memory. By the time she was betrothed at seventeen, her one concern was to hide from Henry the fact that she was not the innocent maid he had a right to expect.'

Bridget paused, as though listening to the bitterness in her own voice. 'Perhaps I am unjust. Poor Mary has paid for her early folly. Five of her eight children were born dead, and I think she regards that as a judgment. Yet she has never been able to see why I shrink from the thought of breeding.

'After my father died, I went to live with her and Henry, and they began at once to choose bridegrooms for me. I kept saying No. I was able to find an astonishing number of faults in everyone who was trotted out for my inspection. Henry became impatient. He wanted me to make a worthy alliance. There were constant quarrels and arguments, even some show of force. I spent the whole of one Christmas locked in a room without a fire on a diet of bread and water.'

'Oh, that was iniquitous! How could they be so cruel?'

'Well, my temper kept me warm! I had a certain relish for my fights with Henry. I am far cleverer than he is, and

I was always able to see through his schemes and outwit him.

'My chief trouble was Mary. She was so conscious of being the cause of my reluctance to marry and so afraid I should one day boil over with rage and tell Henry why. I didn't know what to do. In the old days I could have entered a convent, but now the only woman allowed to remain a virgin is the Queen. Then I had an idea. I was twenty years old, and I thought that if I appealed to the Court of Wards I should be allowed to take my fortune and live unmolested in the house of one of my married friends. The next thing I knew, I had been placed under the guardianship of Sir William Rydal, who was seeking a bride for his heir. I was near to despair!'

'You never showed it. You were altogether splendid, caring for me and giving me courage without letting slip a hint of your own anxieties.'

'I had to put on a brave face. I was determined to play all the tricks I had already practised on Henry. Though when I saw Martin for the first time, I admit my heart sank. It was hard to think of any objection to such a bridegroom—so handsome, so talented and so much liked.'

In spite of everything, Lucy could not help a quiver of pride and pleasure at this description.

'I treated him disgracefully,' said Bridget. 'I wanted to make him dislike me, so that he would be the one to cry off. And luckily he had the good sense to see that you would suit him far better. Though I don't think he has ever entirely forgiven me.'

'He has never understood you. We none of us have.'

'Small wonder! Who ever heard of a woman who was too faint-hearted to bear children? But I kept my own counsel, seized my chance and married William. Not out of greed, but from a craven desire to escape my natural fate. I am glad he never guessed the truth, for it would have hurt him deeply. I hope I made him a good wife while he lived. When he died, I became my own mistress, and neither my kinsfolk nor the Court of Wards can ever force me to take another husband.'

Bridget moved slightly, and Lucy was able to see how haggard she looked, as though she had not slept for nights on end.

She said, 'I thought I need never again face the necessity of watching a woman in labour. If I had known that Agnes was with child, I would have contrived somehow, arranged for her lying-in without being present. Yesterday I was caught off my guard. I saw history repeating itself, that little simpleton in the same plight as Mary. I flew into a panic, and that's why I was so heartless and unkind to Agnes, and why I deserted you at such a moment. I'm sorry, Lucy.'

'It's of no consequence.' Lucy sat upright in the bed and drew up her knees. 'Did Agnes tell you who it was got her with child?'

Bridget related the drear little story, which Lucy heard without any particular emotion, for she had already acquitted Giles in her own mind once she heard the real reason for Bridget's strange behaviour. They both fell into a thoughtful silence. Lucy had discovered that she was feeling hungry, and was wondering whether it would sound callous to say so, when Bridget spoke again in a low uncertain voice.

'Agnes is well enough, thanks to you, but my contemptible fears have driven me into something far worse. If you did but know how I despise myself!'

She got up with a blundering impatience, as if she could no longer keep still, moved away from the window and came to rest near the dressing-chest where she began to fiddle with the pins and combs. Lucy wondered what else she could have on her conscience. Some other luckless young woman rejected in an hour of need? It was hard to hear what Bridget was saying, but the phrases did not seem to tally.

'I led him on deliberately . . . he knew it . . . and then played the pious hypocrite to cover my own weakness . . .'

Enlightenment came with a sense of freezing calm.

'You are speaking of Giles. You are in love with him!'

'Heaven knows why! He is the last man on earth I should have chosen, and he is not even handsome. Yet I am drawn to him as a compass-needle flies to the north. When I am with him, I cannot take my eyes from him. When I am without him, I can think of no one else.'

'I know,' said Lucy softly.

Bridget came out of her self-absorbing trance. 'Forgive me? I have become too wrapped in my own misfortunes. You are the last person I should confide in.'

'There is no need to be so scrupulous. I have no special claim to be sheltered from the truth.' Lucy was determined to behave well. 'I should like to hear what has happened. Giles asked you to marry him and you refused him—for the same reason you have refused so many others?'

'Yes. Only this time it was different. I had a desperate longing to give in. And he guessed.'

He would, thought Lucy.

'I could not tell him the story of my abominable cowardice, so I pretended I did not trust him.'

'I dare say many women might have given the same reason. He has not much to complain of.'

'He didn't complain. He sounded humble. Stricken. It wasn't simply his affection I called in question. I acted as though he was a common adventurer who wanted to plunder my inheritance. I was hateful. And now he is going to leave Wansdown, the first house he ever owned, that he is so proud of, and go off and fight in the wars. If he is killed, it will be my fault.'

Lucy saw that she was crying. She had never seen Bridget in tears. If she had wept for Sir William, she had done so in privacy. She did not indulge her soundless grief for long.

Drying her eyes, she said with a quiet desolation, 'You cannot think how much I envy you, Lucy. Whatever you may have done, it is better to accept love than to deny it.'

Lucy was grappling for a reply when Margery Millard looked in at the door.

'Your pardon, madam. I did not know her ladyship was still with you.'

'Don't go,' said Bridget. 'I shan't detain Mrs Rydal any longer.'

She left the room at once, perhaps thankful to end such a revealing interview.

Margery glanced round, opened the livery cupboard, and saw the jug of ale and the trencher of fresh bread she had placed in there the night before.

'Why, madam, you have had no breakfast! You must be so hungry, I wonder her ladyship did not think of it. I did not like to come in before.'

Lucy's appetite had vanished in the last few minutes, though she tried to eat and drink a little. When her maid Deborah came in, she asked for her riding-dress to be laid out and a message sent to the stables. Bay Banneret was to be brought round in half an hour.

She had decided what to do and it had to be done quickly, before her resolution gave way.

As Lucy peered into the low dark entrance of the manor house, she found a number of half-filled chests blocking her way and the servants taking the tapestry off the walls. Giles, in his shirtsleeves, was directing them.

'What are you doing here?' he asked rather un-graciously. He was not at all pleased to see her.

Lucy mastered the disabling kick of emotion she still felt when she saw him, and said, 'I have to talk to you, Sir Giles.'

It was clear that Giles did not want to be talked to, but the servants were looking on and he could not refuse.

'Come in here,' he said, and led the way into the downstairs parlour.

This too was in the process of being dismantled. His heavy Spanish silver had been put away.

'So it's true you are leaving,' she said.

'If that is what brought you here, Lucy, I'm sorry, but you should not have come. I promised Martin . . .'

'If Martin knew why I was here, he would not object. I have come to speak to you of Bridget.'

Until now Giles had been uncomfortable but self-possessed, not wishing to hurt her but having the advantage that she could not hurt him. Now that was changed.

A shutter came down behind his eyes as he demanded, 'What has Bridget been telling you?'

'That you asked her to marry you, and she refused.'

'So she boasted to you of her triumph? I own that surprises me. I had not thought her so thick-skinned. Or am I mistaken? Did it please you to know what a fool I have made of myself?'

Lucy realised that this was someone she had never seen before: Giles in the grip of a genuine, painful and disappointed love. She doubted whether any other woman had ever reduced him to this state. He had come to think himself invincible. He was being paid back in his own coin, and perhaps it served him right. Yet, hearing the raw misery in his voice, she could not prevent a stirring of compassion.

She said evenly, 'It does not please me to see you so unhappy. And Bridget is unhappy, too. You have not understood—that is to say, she did not tell you—her true reason for sending you away. It is a very strange reason, which I think you ought to know, for it explains a great deal.'

'What do you mean, Lucy? What better reason can there be than her perfectly natural distrust of every promise I made her?'

'She has an overpowering dread of bearing children.'

He stared at her, uncomprehending, and she had a sudden misgiving that he might not be able to make allowances, might despise and condemn such an unnatural weakness. 'In which case,' she thought, 'I am doing Bridget a great disservice.'

'You don't know what you're saying,' he rapped out. 'Bridget is not afraid of anything. She is the bravest woman I know.'

'She's afraid of this. And with good cause. At least I think so, and I hope you will agree. Even though her fears may be irrational.'

And she told him what had happened to Bridget when she was seven years old.

She need not have doubted his response. Compassion blazed up consuming all his rancour and self-pity.

'Poor Bridget,' he kept saying. 'Poor child. What she must have gone through. And no one she could turn to—least of all that weak-willed sister who ought to have protected her out of common gratitude. She didn't care how much Bridget was badgered and tormented all those years, so long as her own false reputation remained as white as snow. I could kill that woman!'

She was surprised to see there were tears in his eyes. He leant his elbows on the table, thinking.

'She didn't ask you to come here?'

'It never entered her head. I doubt she would have confided in me, only she was driven into a corner yesterday. She drove over to Waldon in her new coach, bringing Agnes with her, who became queasy on the journey and soon afterwards suffered a miscarriage. Bridget behaved very oddly, would have nothing to do with the delivery and left it all to me. This morning she felt obliged to tell me why. She was seized with panic, and could not bear to stay in the sickroom.'

There was no need to tell Giles of her own suspicions at the time; they had faded into irrelevance.

'What am I to do?' He sounded unusually helpless.

'Come and see her at the great house. She will be with us for as long as we have to keep Agnes in bed. I shall make everything plain to Martin.'

'She may not want to see me,' he said doubtfully.

'Yes, she will. Even if she puts up a show of reluctance. She loves you.'

'I thought so once,' he said in a low voice, adding, 'It might be kinder to leave her alone. She has refused me, for whatever reason, and I have no more right to go on pestering her than any of those other louts.'

He had turned a little aside, so that she was able to watch that familiar, well-loved face, the dark brows, the firmness of the mouth that could melt so easily into laughter, the crisp line of the chin and beard. She was aware of a curious change in herself. Seeing him so cast-down did not exactly diminish him in her eyes, yet somehow it seemed to diminish the brightness of the thoughts she had been weaving about him all this time. She had been prepared to see him happy with another woman, for she would be able to remember that she had made him happy too, and had let him go only from a sense of duty. But this was different, unexpected. The sight of his deep unhappiness brought home a sharp comparison. She never had, nor could have, made him feel what he now felt for Bridget. This was his reality, from which she was excluded.

He roused himself to say, 'I'll think over your advice. Whether I take it or not, it was generous of you to come, Lucy. Not many women would have done so in the circumstances.'

'Why not? You cannot suppose that I want you to live as an anchorite for the rest of your life, merely to feed my vanity.'

She was surprised to hear how plausible her words sounded.

'I have done you a great wrong,' he said looking carefully away from her. 'And Martin, too. I hope he is not unkind to you.'

'Not in the least.'

It was to be assumed that the wrong was entirely connected with Martin and his well-justified jealousy, and had nothing to do with breaking her heart.

'He is such a good fellow,' Giles persisted. 'He will come round in the end, if you have patience.'

'I am sure of it.'

He had come round, to the extent of treating her with consideration, bringing her in from the rain, ordering warming-pans and hot milk. She was hardly entitled to ask for more. Torn between the two of them, Lucy had lost everything, thrown away both the substance and the shadow of love, hardly knowing which was which.

She stood up. Her legs felt as though they were stuffed with feathers.

'I must go. I wish you good luck with Bridget.'

He rose, too, and offered to escort her back to Waldon, but that was a mere courtesy, for he knew she would not accept. He came round the side of the table and kissed her gently on the cheek.

'God bless you, dearest Lucy.'

Then he walked with her to the stables, and in the end she was glad to leave him, so that she could ride up quietly into the woods, enduring her sense of desolation and thankful that she had not disgraced herself.

Martin saw her coming a long way off.

He had gone out early as usual, and when he returned and asked for his wife, he had been told that she had gone over to Wansdown, for she had made no secret of where she was going.

The news came as a shock. Last night she had convinced herself that Giles had deceived her, and she had appeared to be almost out of her mind, standing like a statue in the drenching rain. Had she gone to confront her former lover, still in that strange mood, hardly accountable for her actions? Martin's instinct was to go at once and fetch her back, yet he could not quite bring himself to admit that she would do anything rash or violent. In this indecisive state of mind he compromised by setting off on foot instead of on horseback. This would give him more time to think.

He was half-way up the hill when a new idea struck him. Lucy knew that Giles was leaving Wansdown. Suppose that was why she had gone there, hoping that he would take her with him? Hurrying up the steep, enclosing lane, Martin's heart was turned to ice and the sweat on his back ran cold with apprehension. It was not just the agonising thought of losing her—though it was odd he should mind this so much, considering how wretched their marriage had become. Worse still was his picture of the life she would lead if Giles were base enough to take her. Cut off from all honourable society, dependent on a man who would soon tire of her, what would become of her in the end?

He pounded on, wishing he had ridden after all. He

must save Lucy, for her own sake, whether she liked it or
not. He was prepared to beg and plead. All notions of
family pride and his honour as a gentleman had ceased to
trouble him.

As he reached the summit of the hill and looked down,
he saw the grey stone manor house and a tiny, mounted
figure coming towards Waldon. It was a fine warm day
after the storm and the sun was drawing up a vaporous
mist from the wet ground. Horse and rider seemed to be
swimming through the haze.

Martin recognised Lucy and his heart expanded with
relief. She was coming home. In his desperate anxiety he
had persuaded himself that she was running away from
him. It now appeared that Giles had too much sense—or
even too much conscience—to take advantage of her
wild infatuation.

Retreating to his own side of the hill and the cover of
the woods, Martin stood under the great oak and watched her coming closer, his heart full of pity. He was going
to let her ride past him, but as she drew level he was so
moved by her look of withdrawn sadness that he spoke
her name without meaning to.

'Lucy!'

Banneret recognised his voice and did not shy, but
Lucy did. She swerved so that she almost came out of the
saddle. Martin ran forward and grasped the reins.

'I'm sorry. I didn't mean to startle you.'

Lucy gave a little gasp, her eyes dilating.

'I did not see you standing there. I have been to the
manor. I hope you are not angry. I had good reason.'

'You went to say goodbye to Giles.'

He would pretend to believe this; it made an excuse
for her going and one he need not cavil at. But Lucy did
not want an excuse.

'No,' she said firmly. 'I went on Bridget's account, to

tell him why she would not marry him. I should not have gone otherwise.'

'When did Bridget refuse him?'

'Last week. I had the whole story from her this morning, which I never should have done if Agnes had not miscarried, so good does come out of evil.'

Martin felt his head was spinning. 'I don't understand.'

'It's a very strange history; I want to tell it to you as soon as I can.' Lucy glanced round. 'Where's your horse?'

'I walked here,' Martin admitted, afraid she might accuse him of spying. 'If there's a strange history, why don't you tell me now?'

He helped her to dismount, with the impersonal care that a man must show to any lady requiring such assistance. Bay Banneret was tethered to one of the lower branches of the great oak. Another lesser giant had blown down during the great storm in July. Lucy went to sit on the fallen trunk. Martin stationed himself a little way along against the scarred column of wood, bone-white where it had cracked away from the roots.

Once again Lucy poured out the story of what had happened to little Bridget Montresor in the tower of Farfield. Martin took longer than Giles to think it over.

'So that was why she married my uncle,' he said at last.

'And why she refused you. She was not moved by ambition or avarice.'

'Well, I have always been grateful for her refusal. But she served you a bad turn, my poor girl.'

'What do you mean?'

'If my uncle's plan had gone as he intended, you would be married to Giles. And that is what you must have been wishing all this past year.'

'You are mistaken,' she said, with a sudden flush of

animation. 'I have been wicked and faithless, so I suppose you will not believe me, but I have never regretted the past. How could I wish our children unborn? And, besides . . .'

She hesitated, and began to scrape off a slither of bark with her fingernail.

'And besides?' he prompted her.

'We should have been ill matched, Giles and I. That is clear to me now. I have been living in a dream, and they say dreams go by opposites.'

Martin remembered her anguish as she said goodbye to Giles under the apple tree. 'I shall feel the same for ever.' He would never let her know that he had overheard that. Even if she was acting now, it was a brave attempt, and he would be a fool to discourage her.

But perhaps she was not acting after all. She had been so very young when he married her, and their wedding had been arranged with such smoothness and speed —once Sir William had realised that this was the best way out of the tangle he had got into with his two heiresses. Lucy had never known any of the secret excitements, the contrasting emotions, of a courtship whose outcome was undecided. Was that why she had fallen a victim to Giles's skill at that exhilarating game? Or had she always foreseen the danger? It was odd to think that she had once regarded him as a usurper in their old home. It hardly mattered any more.

He moved a little closer. Her head was bent as she went on peeling the bark from the tree. He could not see her face.

He said, 'Look at me, Lucy.'

She raised her eyes obediently, those violet-blue eyes, as sad and beseeching now as they had been when he first discovered their beauty in the walled garden five years ago.

She encountered a gaze of strong and searching tenderness she had half forgotten and never expected to see again.

She held out her hands in a clumsy gesture and scrambled to her feet, almost falling against him. There was no need to speak. They clung together, finding hope and comfort.

Bridget had taken refuge in the small banqueting-room which led out of the long gallery and looked down on the enclosed garden. In spite of her preoccupation, she had noticed at dinner that there was a renewed intimacy between Lucy and Martin. They seemed to be speaking direct to each other, instead of to some invisible person a few feet away. So she had decided to make herself scarce. She had gone dutifully to visit Agnes, but Agnes was asleep, so she had retreated in here, feeling a fish out of water in a house that had once been her own, and having nothing to do but brood over her own folly.

This was where Giles found her.

He had felt a certain diffidence about calling at Waldon Harbour, and had sent a message to Martin to say he was here.

Instead of delivering it, the man fetched John Redfern, who came to greet him with a punctilious bow reserved for honoured friends of the family.

'Good day, Sir Giles. May I conduct you upstairs while they go to find Mr Rydal?'

'No!' Giles spoke with a peremptory snap because he was nervous. 'Find Mr Rydal first, and I will wait here.'

Redfern bowed once more and took himself off, looking injured.

Giles stood in the great hall. Like Bridget, he too had once lived in this house and now felt a stranger. He stared at the dais where, in Sir William's time, the family had dined at the high table while the servants ate their meal at two long trestles on the lower level, a custom which had terrified Lucy and must have seemed very old-fashioned to Bridget, though she had never tried to alter any of her husband's settled habits. He thought about Bridget's curious first marriage, and was taken by surprise when Martin came up behind him.

'Well, Giles?'

He swung round.

'You may wonder at my being here. I thought it best to send word . . .'

'I was expecting you. Lucy tells me that you wish to see Bridget.'

'You don't object?'

'Why should I?' said Martin pleasantly.

He looked different. The grim lines round his mouth had gone. All the same, Giles could not help thinking that he himself might no longer be acceptable to Martin as the second husband of his uncle's extremely wealthy widow. He mumbled something indistinct.

'My dear Giles, are you asking for my blessing on your courtship? You surely cannot believe that I could stop Bridget marrying you if she once made up her mind to it, even supposing I wished to! Which I don't. And, if you are wise, you won't let her guess that you ever thought of asking my opinion, or she will be highly incensed with us both.'

Giles laughed. He couldn't help it. Martin laughed, too, and they eyed each other with a revival of old sympathies.

Giles thought, 'Please God, I shall soon be able to meet him without this damnable weight of guilt.'

When he entered the small banqueting-room and found Bridget sitting there so forlorn, he realised that here at least his transgressions no longer counted. It was in her earlier life, not his, that the barrier between them was rooted.

She looked up as the door opened and saw him poised on the threshold, regarding her with his dark gaze. She was surprised and confused. She had felt safe from Giles at Waldon Harbour.

'Does Martin know you are here?'

'I've just spoken with him. It was you I came to see. My dear, why could you not tell me?'

'Tell you what?'

'The reason you will not marry again.'

She tore her eyes from his and stared down at her fingers knotted in her lap. She was beginning to tremble.

'Granted, you were not obliged to give a reason, but when you said you would not trust me . . .'

'I never meant that. It was a hateful lie.'

'I only wish you could have trusted me enough to confide in me as a friend. Perhaps you think such matters ought not to be mentioned between a man and a woman, yet you were never one to hide the truth behind an apron of fig-leaves.'

Bridget was now fully enlightened.

'So Lucy went running to you! I might have known she would betray me.'

'Now don't speak unkindly of Lucy. She has been a good angel to us both. My dear, what were you afraid of? Your sister's reputation is safe with me—though I shan't attempt to tell you what I think of the way she and her husband have treated you, for I dare say you would be offended. But all that is beside the point. You have done nothing to be ashamed of.'

He sat down beside her and tried to take her hands. She pulled away and would not look at him.

'You are not angry with me for wanting to comfort you?'

'Oh no! Only with myself. And as for being ashamed —can you not see how humiliating it is that you, of all people, should learn of my contemptible weakness? A soldier, a man who scaled the walls of Cadiz with Essex.'

'Good God, what has this to do with Essex?'

'You are a hero, and I have been such a coward.'

'I don't see the comparison,' he said thoughtfully. 'I'd rather attack a city than endure the rigours of child-birth.'

'So should I,' said Bridget, and laughed reluctantly when he did.

Though he could see what the trouble was. Proud, independent Bridget who could hold her own in a man's world—oversee an estate, school her own horses, build an almshouse, manage her own finances—how galling it must be for her to know that, when it came to the role for which women were chiefly valued, she was unable to compete with gentle Lucy or foolish Agnes. He felt the deepest pity for her and knew that he must never show it.

'If you are determined to think ill of yourself,' he said bracingly, 'remember that you don't hold a monopoly in self-abasement. How do you think I felt when you found me skulking behind the arras and helped me to escape from your house in the middle of the night? You commanded me to visit you next day. I knew that you despised me, and rightly. Coming back to the Priory was the hardest thing I ever had to do.'

'Was it?' she asked, her interest kindling. 'I was so enraged with you, though I soon began to like you better, for you were honest, you never tried to shift the blame. Or put on the peacock airs of a successful lover, as some men might have done.'

'I should not have dared,' he said, smiling.

This time when he tried to take her in his arms, she did not resist but returned his kisses passionately, responding with all the eagerness and vitality in her nature. In fact it was Giles who was the first to call a halt, gently untwining her arms and setting a little distance between them.

'How long shall you remain here? May I come and see you at the Priory before I leave?'

'But you aren't going away now?' she asked in dismay.

'Dear heart, I think I must. I can't continue living so near you, feeling as I do and knowing that nothing can come of it. Kissing and embracing is very well to start with—what Sidney called the breakfast of love—only I should soon want more, and then I should grow cross and I dare say we should quarrel.'

'I don't understand. Don't you still want to marry me?'

She was as puzzled as a hurt child. 'Have you changed your mind since finding out what a coward I have been?'

'You know I want to marry you, Bridget. But not at the cost of causing you intolerable anguish. And though I don't want to sound a coxcomb, I think if I remained here you might in time be tempted to break your life-long resolution, if only to stop me from plaguing you. I don't wish to marry you on those terms and then see you suffering torments of fear every time we lay together, in case I got you with child.'

'I shouldn't suffer torments,' she protested. 'Truly I should not. Good God, how am I to convince you, after all my years of folly? The case is altered. I want a child, which I never did before. Your child. I was never in love until now. That's the difference.'

Her warped and exaggerated fear of childbearing had held her for years in a cruel trap. The one instinct strong enough to exorcise that fear would always have been a natural and healthy love for a man who wanted to marry her and give her children. And because the secret dread had been with her long before she came to maturity, she had trained herself to shut her heart automatically against anyone who came to her in the guise of a suitor. Only after refusing Giles had she fully recognised the violent contradiction in her feelings. Even then, she might not have been able to break the spell. It was her confession to Lucy which had finally set her free.

'Through all those years of silence,' she said, 'I dared not confide in anyone. And then, this morning, when I tried to describe my sister's miscarriage, it suddenly came to me how puny my old terrors were, like all the hideous nightmares of childhood. I've harboured my nightmare far too long, but I'll be rid of it now! You won't have a fainting, squeamish wife, I promise you, Giles. Can you believe me?'

Her eyes were wide and imploring.

'I believe you, sweetheart.'

He kissed her again, thinking how little he deserved his reward. If he had acted as everyone expected him to, paid court to Sir William's widow as soon as it was decent, she would have armed her defences against him also, and he would probably have got no further than the others. As it was, he had perfidiously seduced the wife of his friend, and Bridget had been so angry with him, so concerned for Lucy, so determined to save her and Martin from the consequences of this rash intrigue, that he himself had assumed an important place in her life before she was aware of it.

'When did you begin to fall in love with me?' he asked curiously.

'I think it was when I saw you lying on the ground and those louts kicking you.'

'An epic scene!'

She laughed at his expression of comical chagrin. 'Where are we going to live?'

'Where should you prefer?'

She considered. 'How would it be if we settled at the Priory while we enlarge Wansdown? Or we could build on some other part of the estate if you would like that better.'

They made plans, with the slightly astonished pleasure of two people who had never expected to play this particular game. Presently they decided to go out into the garden.

As they emerged from the banqueting-room, they saw Martin and Lucy at the other end of the gallery. Both couples were frozen by a momentary awkwardness. Giles bit his lip. Lucy cast a glance of mute appeal at Martin. Then Bridget felt for Giles's hand and pressed it hard. Martin slipped a protective arm round Lucy.

Like musicians playing in consort, they were all ready to be done with an old tune and start up a new one. Relinquishing the past, they stepped resolutely forward to face each other and the rest of their lives.

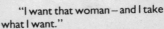